THE COUNTRY WESTERN CORPSE

BY CHARLENE TORKELSON

This book is dedicated to all the dancers I have met, all the dancers I have danced with, and all those I have taught. In some form or another you are a part of this book. A piece of you is in each and every character and in each dance performed. You are a special group of people with unique talents. You have and always will be a part of my life. Since the first year I began ballroom dancing, I have worn a small gold band on my little finger signifying my dedication and connection to all the dancers in the world. This book is for all of you who have played such a significant role in my life. Thank you.

Introduction:

Papa's was huge. The parking lot itself was mammoth in size but once a person entered the double doors at the end of the sloping walk ramp, the inside was breathtaking. Wide open and barely anything in the space other than a small stage along one side wall and a counter along the other side with tall bar stools perched beneath. The low lights made it difficult to even see all the way across the smooth wooden dance floor to the other side of the room. It was all dance floor.

Normally, the music was blasting with dancers dressed in pointy cowboy boots and a few classic Stetsons towering above the height of the crowd. People clapping and laughing and stomping to the beat of the twanging guitar was the typical evening. Normally, this was a place where a person couldn't see across the room because there were too many people crowded into the space. Tonight was different.

Tonight the room was empty except for a few uniformed police peering into the corners of the darkened room and a team of medics lifting a body onto a gurney. The ceiling fans swung around and around above with low swishing sounds. Heads shook in puzzled disbelief as the body traveled across the glistening dance floor and out the double doors into the acre of black top – now empty except for a few black and white squad cars and an ambulance. It was now four o'clock in the morning and still an inky black evening sky. What exactly had happened in the hours before this person now dead had been laughing and dancing? And who was this mysterious cowboy who died with his dancing boots on?

I.

KiKi Mays climbed out of her older rusted sedan and strutted confidently toward the mall entrance. She glanced at the glistening glass in the door and smiled. Her new look was smart and exciting. She stopped to touch the new close cropped hair at the nape of her neck. It was different. She had to admit it would take some time to get used to. Her usual puffy halo of kinky black hair had been chopped close to her head with a tight cluster of curls right in the front above her forehead. That would show him!

Kiki hadn't been at the dance studio for several days. She had called in sick after finding out charming Clive Forbes, her supposed boyfriend was neither charming nor her boyfriend. Both tall handsome Clive and exotic KiKi were ballroom dance teachers at the studio centering the upscale mall in an upper class suburb of Minneapolis. If you asked anyone in the studio they would tell you it was assumed Kiki and Clive were a couple. If you asked Clive, however, the answer would be quite different. Clive had explained to Kiki in his charming yet degrading way that he couldn't be tied down to any one person. That had put Kiki into a tailspin crying binge lasting for days. Clive would certainly feel arrogant about the affect he had on Kiki as it was the same one he thought he had on all women he knew. She would show him. She finally got herself together after a few days of holing up in her tiny efficiency apartment, went out and got an expensive haircut that she couldn't afford then dressed in a particularly slinky dress and headed back to the studio.

Walking past the front desk with a new spring in her step, Kiki Mays waved at the receptionist and strolled into the teachers' office. Little did she know this studio would soon suffer the effects of a murder – and unfortunately for Kiki, the victim wouldn't be Clive Forbes.

Ashley Arthur sat poised at his desk, the first one in the long line of cupboards and counters that made up the teachers' office for the dance studio. The office was long and narrow giving only enough space on each side for counter and chairs pushed in beneath. If two teachers were actually seated back to back, they would certainly collide — it was that narrow.

Ashley glanced up as Kiki strutted past. Then he took a second look, noticing her new hair and stunning appearance. Not that he was drawn to her looks in a romantic way. Women were not his passion, but he did appreciate style. "You look fabulous, darling!" he gushed straightening his round glasses on his chubby cheeked face.

Kiki nodded with a knowing smile and pushed past him to her desk located in the center of the right side of the room. She twirled and touched her new hair behind her ear. "You like?" She moved with incredible grace even in the tight quarters of this cramped office space.

He nodded and smiled. Then he snorted. His mind had moved beyond the new appearance to the reason behind the change. Clive Forbes was not one of his favorite people. It was too bad someone had to look so good for someone like Clive. He didn't want to wait around to witness the confrontation between the two, so he got up and left the room with his dance program in hand. He would find a space out on the dance floor to finish his daily lesson preparation. His stomach turned at the thought of Clive's reaction. It turned even more when he considered Kiki would once again get sucked into Clive's harem with a sweet comment or two from the snake's evil mouth about her new and stunning look. She would blush then rush back into his arms reuniting the sweet princess with the monster. It was sickening. Ashley shuddered at the thought.

Clive Forbes strutted in with his usual arrogance. He was tall and lean. At about six feet three inches tall, he was probably the tallest of the studio's male teachers. His black hair was combed back and stylishly longer on the sides and back. Ashley couldn't help but notice the line of hair along his forehead was beginning to slowly move back a bit especially for someone so young. At twenty one years old, Clive was a few years younger than the mid twenty year old Kiki Mays. But Clive had a more mature appearance than someone else of his age. His features were those of his father — a well known scientist of Middle Eastern heritage. Clives' nose was Greek-like and his skin olive in color. His black eyes glistened when they narrowed giving his bushy black eyebrows a furrowed look. Those brows frequently touched in the center when he frowned – which lately was often. That look was very controlling especially to women it appeared for he had a following of beauties who seemed to hang on his every word wherever he walked.

Today, Clive wore a stylish crisp white shirt with an untied narrow tie hanging loosely around his neck. His black pants were shiny and of a crinkled popular disco fabric that narrowed around his ankles. He wore a pair of slip on black shoes of soft leather in a textured pattern. Although most dancers wore special dance shoes when teaching, Clive sometimes wore his street shoes because they were made similar to the soft soled dance shoe. He made sure of that. With a black jacket slung over his shoulder he strutted in, stopped briefly at the desk to check for messages and a quick look at his schedule for the day, and walked right past Ashley without so much as a nod of acknowledgement. Ashley always hated that about Clive. He rarely took note of the men, only the women.

Ashley waited a few minutes for the confrontation he knew would take place in the teachers' office between Kiki and Clive. Puffing out his cheeks and letting the air out in a huff, he considered the possibilities. The two would make up and arm in arm sachet out to the dance floor for a romantic Rumba. It would be sickening. Or maybe it wouldn't end quite so sweetly. He smirked at this possibility.

Ashley's chocolate skin was considerably lighter than Kiki's, but staring at himself in the floor to ceiling mirror along the wall he lifted his posture and turning his head from side to side admired his clean cut appearance. Ashley normally walked as tall as his small stature allowed. As a dancer, he wanted his five foot four inches to seem tall and powerful — which of course it never was. His body was a bit too flabby and soft for that. Lifting his chin, he strutted to the corner to turn on the music. That way if there was a fight, anyone in the reception area would miss at least most of the high pitched yelling and screaming.

To his surprise, Kiki waltzed out of the office alone. She had a confident sneer on her face as she picked up a few dance folders from the corner holder and proceeded to flutter toward the back ballroom. Clive came out of the office with a puzzled look on his face, then spotting Ashley staring at him regained his confident expression. But clearly, Clive had not won this battle, and it upset him. His eyebrows remained in a confused scowl with the inner tips almost meeting.

Normally late, at least later than the rest of the studio staff, owner Edward Garrett was unusually early on this particular day. Owning two studios in the Minneapolis area, he preferred to stay in the downtown studio as it was nearer his high-rise condo. He wasn't one who enjoyed the travel. But today he was clearly agitated. Something had brought him out to the suburban studio, and it was not good news.

Edward, sometimes referred by the staff behind his back as Eddie G, muttered to himself as he approached the tall reception desk just beyond the reception area. About six feet tall, Edward Garrett had a mass of curly hair that was the butt of many a joke. It was a toupee – one of three that he owned showing various stages of length. First, was the fresh haircut stage, then the medium grown out stage, and finally the "needs a cut" stage. The toupee obviously was a concern as he frequently stared at himself as he passed a mirror and adjusted it when it wasn't quite straight. In a studio with walls of mirrors, this was a frequent occurrence.

Today, Edward wore a well tailored suit of white with a lightly abstract patterned shirt in a pastel shade and a white tie. Everything Edward Garrett owned was immaculate in cut and style. However, it was also something that stood out in a crowd. And Edward definitely stood out in a crowd. Whether from his attire or his flamboyant personality, he was a man who was noticed anywhere he went. Yes, Edward Garrett was a man of charisma. Unfortunately, it wasn't always the good that drew people to him. He was a man of talent both in dancing and in creativity, but he was also a man with many vices. Basically, any vice you could imagine was or had been one of Edward Garrett's downfalls at one time or another. He was a man who went into something with all his heart and soul – and it wasn't always for the best. Today, he was dealing with something difficult, and the staff at this studio would soon be dealing with that difficulty as well.

II.

Gathering the group of about six staff members into the small ballroom for the daily meeting, Edward Garrett slid across the floor from office door to table in about three long strides. Although he had arrived earlier before most of the staff, he was still late to the meeting. There was a saying in the studio, "There is real time and there is Edward Garrett time." Obviously the two were never the same. Some thought the reason Edward was always late was to make a memorable entrance. Others thought it was because he just didn't care — others' time just wasn't important enough to consider. That was probably the truth of the matter. Edward didn't care about anyone else unless it was to benefit Edward Garrett. Then he was a most generous person if it provided something he wanted. Yes, Edward had his moments of being benevolent and giving. Those were the times that confused people most. Just asking the question "why?" was something to ponder carefully if you were the recipient of his generous nature.

Seated at the head of the table, Edward began his usual nervous tapping on the table with his fingertips as studio manager Joan Ericson went over the daily schedule. Then just when she was to start with her planned agenda, he began to bounce his knees up and down nervously as if waiting for his turn to speak or

7

possibly he needed a trip to the restroom very badly. He became easily bored with anyone else's report. Finally, Joan turned to him and said, "Do you have something to say, Mr. Garrett?" in as polite a voice as possible. Joan was patiently used to this behavior.

Joan Ericson had been with the studio for years. First as a student, then a teacher and a receptionist, and finally when the staff had upped and quit on a payroll issue, Edward had reluctantly made her the studio manager. No longer the youthful slight teen with the big smile and even more prominent dimples she was when she began, Joan was now a matronly woman with a round face and just as round a body. But those dimples remained – they would always remain. Edward considered her overweight appearance to be detrimental to the dance industry and certainly not the correct persona for one meeting and greeting new students, but her competence had been overwhelming. The studio began to flourish when Joan Ericson had taken over this position, so he begrudgingly had conceded defeat. After all, money was a huge motivator for Edward Garrett. And Joan Ericson was making him money.

With the invitation to speak, Edward hopped up and began to pace the floor. "We have a situation," Edward began. The eyes all turned to stare at him waiting for him to continue. He paced a few more steps and then turned with a stare that wasn't at anyone in particular.

"We have a situation," he repeated with his pointer finger shaking in front of his face. "Not here in this studio, but certainly one that will affect this location." He took in a deep breath. "The downtown studio is losing its lease." The eyes began to look around at each other with curiosity.

8

Edward Garrett had first begun his dance business with a studio in the downtown Minneapolis area. It was originally in the lower level of a parking ramp. Situated perfectly for years within eyesight immediately when the elevator to the ramp opened, the downtown studio had been the focal point of anyone and everyone who drove downtown to work. They had to spot the studio as they came in every morning and had to pass it when they left each night. The success of that studio had been the catalyst for this studio out in the suburbs. For years the two had worked out well. Then the parking ramp had begun a renovation, and the downtown studio had been forced to move to a huge overpowering space vacated by a large department store across the street. Although spacious for dancing, it was perhaps too much space and certainly overpriced. The rent was always a monthly issue not only for the studio downtown, but for the studio in the suburbs who had to make up any differences in income to pay the exuberant rent and payroll accrued by the staff downtown.

The eyes said all that needed to be said. "What now? What more can happen to us?" A new staff still training to become a prize staff, they had heard all the disaster stories from the previous staff about this situation. What could they expect now?

Edward continued. "We have found a space to relocate…". Everyone breathed a sigh of relief. Then he continued again. "It is a smaller space located in an up and coming mall just north of the downtown area." They all smiled. That sounded very good. "The rent is definitely much better." Again they smiled. "The floor is a bit small…". His voice trailed, and they frowned, but just a little bit. A smaller dance floor than the huge space currently occupied?

That didn't sound too bad. After all, it wasn't their staff downsizing.

Edward began to pace. "But we are not able to get into that space for another two months while the mall is being completed. So that studio—staff and students—are coming out here for about two months to share this space with you."

The looks began to flutter anxiously, and Joan Ericson, usually a calm person, began to glare. This news was obviously news to her as well. Let's see. Two staffs sharing the narrow tiny staff office space. Two staffs fighting for lesson space in the two ballrooms each hour. This was going to be tight.

Edward was not quite finished with his news. "In addition, because of the financial obligations we will have at this point in time with the move and all—remodeling—we will schedule our upcoming dance showcase here in this studio rather than the normal hotel setting we are used to. We can't afford the expense of the hotel."

This last announcement just about sent Joan Ericson through the ceiling. Her mouth gaped open in shock before she rose and asked for an immediate closed door meeting with Edward to further discuss this whole situation. While the two of them scurried into his office across from the reception desk, the staff put on some music and began to dance. "When all else fails — dance" was the motto of the studio. And all else was certainly failing right now.

Kiki Mays swiveled toward Ashley Arthur and asked him to dance. He pulled back a bit covering his mouth in exaggerated shock, but she only laughed at his antics. Then Molly Ross and

Tommy McLaufflin snagged each other leaving Clive Forbes to stand sulking in the corner watching the two couples move elegantly across the floor to a piece of Waltz music.

When Joan and Edward emerged, there were no happy shining faces but rather two people who had agreed to some rather unfortunate compromises. Edward was stone faced and angry — not at Joan, but at the situation. Joan was trying to make the best of a difficult event and looked around the studio with new eyes imagining the influx of staff and students. Her mouth was grim but she eyed each corner and pursed her lips envisioning what would and what would not be shared.

III.

Molly Ross was tiny. Not waiflike by any means, but maybe short was a better word than tiny. Molly, not even five feet tall, was solid and busty. Her dark almost black hair flowed back from her face with a slight bit of wave – thick and luxurious. She would hurry into the studio each day with no make-up and a baggy sweatshirt covering her long black skirt, carrying a blouse on a hanger in one hand and a satchel like purse in the other. Although young, she had already been married for three years to her high school sweetheart. She never wore a wedding band nor a diamond on her finger, and no one seemed even remotely aware what this husband's name was much less what he looked like. The one thing they did know was he worked nights. Molly was always trying to find something to do at the end of the studio night rather than return to an empty home. Want to go out dancing at a disco?

11

Molly was up for it. Maybe a bite to eat? Yup, Molly would be happy to come along.

Kiki Mays really needed a friend tonight. In spite of looking in complete control of the situation with Clive, inside she was a basket case. So when she looked across at Molly Ross sitting hunched over her time slip busily trying to figure out the numbers by adding on her fingers, she knew she could count on her for an evening out. "Say Molly, how about going out dancing tonight?"

Molly looked up from her work and without missing a beat and suggested a new dance club to the south of the studio called "Papa's". "It's something that is really getting big now. It's got country western music." Molly's large brown eyes seemed enormous on her face. They were edged in heavy black eyeliner with an extra coating of mascara on her long lashes.

Of course Kiki Mays would have said "yes" to just about any suggestion. So with a slight frown at the words "country western" she eagerly agreed to the plans. Tommy McLaufflin looked over from his desk space tucked in the back corner of the office. "I'm up for it," he agreed twirling in his desk chair.

Tommy was a new teacher just as Molly was. He looked more like a football player than a dancer. Leaning back in his chair, his feet propped up showed his stark white dance shoes. For some unusual reason, after Tommy found this pair of rather cheap white dance shoes at a local shoe store, all the male dancers in the studio as well as many of the students decided to buy the exact same pair of shoes. It had become a signature of the studio — white dance shoes for the men. Tommy was a young handsome man with a beach bum tanned face and sun bleached blond hair and matching mustache. His face was "cute" rather than handsome like Clive Forbes. Although Tommy and Clive were friends through their dancing, they were also rather competitive rivals. Each wanted to outdo the other in everything. Sometimes it became rather annoying for the rest of the studio staff. This showoff mentality could be trying when watching two young twenty year olds facing off on the dance floor.

Kiki glanced over at Tommy. "Great, let's all go as soon as Molly is done with her work."

Both Kiki and Tommy stared immediately at Molly who dropped the work paper back onto her desk and jumped up to change her shoes. Her ruffled blouse belted at the waist might not really fit into a cowboy bar, but she didn't seem to mind as she leaned down to unhook the straps on her black Latin shoes and slip into a pair of mid calf well-worn black boots.

The three were impressed with the size of the dance floor at Papa's. At first Tommy danced with one woman and then the other woman, but soon both Tommy and Molly became tired of Kiki's sullen moodiness and constant chatter about Clive Forbes and eventually convinced a friend of a friend to sit with her for the continuation of the sob story. Then after a few dances Molly and Tommy left together. Kiki had about exhausted her shoulders to cry on and left alone for a gloomy drive back to her tiny apartment. At least she had gotten through the day. Her smudged mascara lined down her cheeks as she drove silently through the darkness.

The next day Clive had begun a new tactic toward Kiki – fight fire with fire. When Kiki arrived trying to look fresh and renewed after a late night of dancing, Clive was already teaching one of his students in the small ballroom past the reception desk. Normally he taught in the reclusive back ballroom, but today he wanted everyone to notice. Wrapped up in his arms was cute blond student named Donnette Hubble. Donnette was a new student with more talent as a dancer than most of the teachers. She moved with confidence and grace, and Clive was making the most of the lesson by leading her in as many advanced steps as he could remember. Donnette giggled and smiled in her charming little girl way. A tiny five feet tall, she had a cheerleader toned body and tightly curled ringlets of blond curls framing her all-American face. She was the girl next door, the little sister everyone wanted to protect, and the object of Clive Forbes' full attention at this moment.

Kiki found herself slowing in pace as she tried to glide through the room unfazed to the teachers' office, but her stare caught her. Clive knew he had hit his mark. He smirked as he lead Donnette into a romantic Rumba cross body lead with an under arm turn left then immediately into a flamboyant cross over with extended arm styling. Donnette matched his every move and swayed her hips suggestively in perfect Latin motion. This seemed a perfectly natural dance for her.

It was unfortunately at that very moment Edward Garrett paced out of his office and took a quick glance across the dance floor. His face went from a scowl to an energetic smile. Crossing the floor with long strides, he reached the dancing couple and extended his hand introducing himself to the blushing Donnette Hubble with an elegant run of compliments. He ended with a "You know Mr. Forbes, I think this lovely young lady would be a perfect candidate for our teacher training program, don't you?" Edward extended his neck as he continued to smile at the confused Donnette. Clive cleared his throat. This would certainly put a crimp in Clive's plans not to mention his paycheck with one less student to teach. If Donnette became a teacher, then his nightmare would really begin. He would have several women right here in the studio all wanting his full attention, and Clive was certainly not willing to give them all his full attention. A woman in every port was sort of Clive's motto. Two or more would cause problems.

"She certainly has the talent, Mr. Garrett," Clive diplomatically agreed. Then he added, "But we are just beginning our lessons. She is a new student who is looking forward to competing in the future. Miss Hubble would love to take a few titles, if you know what I mean." Clive flashed a smile at Donnette who gazed up into his face and nodded. She loved the idea of being a star just as Clive had told her so many times. He had built the dream already in her mind. Twirling around the floor in a lovely dance dress with the crowd clapping wildly was an image she relived over and over on each lesson she took. Clive had painted a glowing picture of her potential opportunities and becoming a teacher hadn't been mentioned.

Edward Garrett scowled but only briefly. Don't let the student see you disagreeing with her beloved teacher. He nodded in agreement and then added, "That's a wonderful goal. Maybe after you've won all the amateur awards, you'll want to consider the professional ones as well." That should get her mind going, he thought but Donnette just looked more confused as she nodded back. Not the brightest bulb, he thought when he realized she had not caught on to his insinuations. He left the dance floor and lounged at the reception desk until the lesson was over, once again complimenting her dancing as she left the studio. At the doorway, Donnette turned to wave a cute little girl flutter at both men who remained side by side smiling back at her. Her short pleated skirt swung as she made a quick about face and out the door.

"You better not be dating her," Edward hissed out of the side of his mouth when she turned back looking over her shoulder with a flash of a smile.

"Of course not," Clive lied. "Do you take me for a fool?"

"Yes." Edward Garrett's word was to the point. He turned on his heel and reentered his office leaving Clive standing at the desk with Kiki Mays glaring at Clive's slightly hunching back. He didn't even need to turn around to know she was there. He could feel the burn.

IV.

Joan Ericson usually waited until the very last minute to leave for the studio. Today she stood in her kitchen, a dated tiny space in an older two story duplex that she shared with her dog. She took a last gulp of coffee and put the empty cup into the sink to wash later. Pacing between the kitchen and the living room as if debating her next move, she finally picked up her large tapestry bag and slung it over her shoulder, looked back at her sleeping dog, and traipsed down the back stairs to her single stall garage. Her navy blue car was sensible just like most of her possessions. Sensible was the best word to describe Joan Ericson. The drive took only ten to fifteen minutes, but it was far enough away to keep her private life secluded.

Today Joan was early to work. She didn't really know why, she just knew she needed time to think. Exiting her car she slowly stared across the parking lot, hoisted her overstuffed bag to her shoulder and looked down at her feet. There was a time when she was a woman who looked like a dancer – not really skinny and sleek because she was normal in her height and not tall like the models Edward Garrett preferred. No, Joan Ericson had not been a beauty, but she had been slender and bubbly with an engaging smile and deep dimples in each cheek. She kept a framed photo on her desk of one of the first shots taken of her in the studio. She was standing with a much younger Edward Garrett and two other teachers. It reminded her of why this place was so special to her.

The image of today's Joan Ericson that she glanced at in the window of the mall door was no longer the young vibrant teacher she had been. Rather she was round and matronly, but she carefully chose her clothes to enhance her figure. Today she wore a stylish black patterned tunic with cranberry and sage paisleys over a black floating skirt that draped to her ankles. And her feet. Her feet were and always would be those of a dancer. They were small and perfectly proportioned with a slight turn out. Always as her first act of the day after entering the studio, Joan would put those beautiful dancing feet into a pair of lovely Latin dance shoes – a strappy pair of black heels with rhinestones on the T-strap. Today was no different. However, on the way to her office, Joan stopped briefly to stare at the studio. Entering the doorway, she stood legs splayed for balance and carefully noticed every inch of the dance studio. First, the narrow reception area with a seventies wallpaper of silver swirls and teal accents and an equally patterned carpet. The décor was definitely dated and too busy now that it was the nineteen eighties. That was old style disco. The couches were contemporary and uncomfortable with thin teal cushions and metal armrests and legs. Most only sat for a moment or two before moving on to the more comfortable plastic stackable chairs. The reception desk was chest high and curved with notices and messages neatly piled on top. Just beyond was the small ballroom with gleaming wood floors and floor to ceiling mirrors. The entire area was narrow – very narrow. How could two studios fit into this space? Two sets of teachers, students, and managers all clamoring for a piece of this narrow space.

Joan's office was at the end of the tiny ballroom area. The door was just to the right of the entryway to the large back ballroom. The back ballroom was spacious but more like a barn. There were no windows and only a few mirrors. Joan's office did have windows however that opened to the back ballroom. She could watch the lessons as she did her paperwork. Today she moved slowly into her office and closed the door. Staring at the framed photo of herself on her desk, she smiled. So many years had passed since that photo was taken and now she was the manager – the one in charge. Sure, she had a new and inexperienced staff, but they had potential. Clive Forbes could be a handful at times, but he was talented and his students loved him. Hmmm. That too could be a problem at times. Kiki Mays was also very talented. There was no one who could dance so smoothly and effortlessly as Kiki. But the baggage she brought. She and Clive were always at each other's throats. Molly Ross was trying hard. Who knew what her life was like away from the studio? She had so many secrets. But she made an effort and was steadily improving. And Tommy McLaughlin might become a good dancer. He and Clive pushed each other to become better and better, but would their rivalry cause strife? Then there was Ashley. He was a wonderful dancer, but his personality sometimes got in the way of his relationships with others. Staff and students alike could be a problem for Ashley Arthur. Joan shook her head. She already had her work cut out for her, and now this. Now she would have to manage with so many others here as well. And the showcase? The showcase would be here. At the hotel they just walked in, held the event and left. Here they would have to set up and take down, plan the food and set up the music. So much more work. Joan closed her eyes and shook her head. But she smiled and her dimples deepened in her cheeks. Carefully she took out a piece of paper and began to take notes under the title "Showcase".

V.

The dance day had started. Clive was dancing in the back ballroom with a student, Kiki was teaching good old Mr. Nelson, and Tommy was practicing his dance patterns in the back corner preparing for his dance test. Ashley was playing music in the front ballroom trying to find a piece for a routine, and Molly was preparing a program at one of the round tables in the small ballroom.

Joan was seated at her desk peering out onto the dance floor. Her mind was racing with all of the new developments. She was imagining all the changes when the downtown studio joined them. This floor would be filled with teachers, students, and... Like a whirlwind tornado, Edward Garrett spun across the floor leading a tall slender blond woman by the arm. Mr. Garrett normally never appeared in the evening hours. Not out at the suburban studio that is. The downtown studio was his location of choice once the lessons began. He liked to stay close to home when it turned dark, so this was an unusual event. Joan glanced out her door when she heard the footsteps pounding across the floor. Edward had a distinctive sound when he walked across floor – a heaviness with his heels and a swishing across the floor from his soft soled shoes, and Joan's ears were always in tuned to that sound. She frowned. The sound was muffled.

Edward Garrett was dressed impeccably as always in a three piece suit. Tonight the suit was a classic gray pinstripe with a pale gray shirt and patterned gray and rose tie. His imported Italian leather shoes were soft and supple but his long strides echoed through the room. Tonight he escorted a long leggy blond who looked very much like a fashion model but without the gaunt emaciated look. No she was different. She had curves – round hips and full breasts with a bit of tone to her legs and thighs. Her china doll pale skin was smooth and accented with a natural yet clearly made-up appearance. The sleek blond of her hair was cut in a crisp asymmetrical bob allowing the longer side to fall across her forehead and right cheek to a point at her chin. She wore a short slender pencil skirt of royal blue topped by a lacy slightly see through blouse with a deep v in the front. Her strappy heels were high making her already tall stature even taller. She appeared to be almost an inch taller than Edward Garrett. It was the clip clop of her heels that made the sound different. It was the soprano high note to the lower tenor of Edward's shoes that made Joan look around and take special notice.

The pair did not stop at Joan's office. They moved noisily into the large ballroom causing the heads of all the occupants to turn and stare. Clive Forbes could hardly contain himself. His mouth gaped open at the sight of such a beautiful woman, and his older more mature student was not pleased by this attention. She gripped his arm firmly and snorted loudly to regain his attention. Of course Edward would never stop a dance lesson to introduce a guest – lessons were money and money was Edward's top priority. He glanced around the room smiling slightly with pride that their entrance had caused this attention, but then gently took the blonde's elbow and guided her back toward the smaller ballroom. This time he entered Joan's office obviously anxious to introduce his guest to someone – anyone.

"Miss Ericson," he began with a charming smile. "This is Elizabeth Tomlinson."

Joan rose from her desk with a polite expression and extended her hand. Elizabeth was young and didn't quite know what to do next, but suddenly she became aware she should shake the hand that was extended. She limply placed her hand in Joan's and tossed her blond bang back away from her eyes revealing a cold stare.

"You have a lovely studio here, Edward," Elizabeth Tomlinson said in a smoky toned voice as a way of implying she knew who was really in charge. Her long dark lashes fluttered and her chin lowered in a coy expression. She turned her full attention to the man next to her.

"Why thank you, Miss Tomlinson," Edward replied puffed slightly with pride. His mustache bristled as his lips turned up into a gloating smile. He always addressed staff and students by their last name as a way of maintaining professionalism in the studio, but to do this to a personal acquaintance was confusing for both Joan and Elizabeth. Elizabeth frowned slightly but then smiled broadly so as not to seem in any way offended by this manner of address. It was evident she was trying to be as accommodating toward the man as possible. Joan caught herself from rolling her eyes. Another bimbo enticed by Edward Garrett's charismatic personality who would only too soon find out who the real Edward was. Joan smiled at the thought.

Edward Garrett again escorted Elizabeth out the door and stood for a moment longer in the doorway to the larger ballroom basking in the stares from Clive and Tommy toward his "guest". Kiki and Mr. Nelson paid no attention at all to either Edward or Elizabeth. Mr. Nelson was a long-time student. A lawyer who was about as mellow and cheerful as a person could be. His wife had no interest in dancing. Actually she had several health issues that prevented her from exerting herself, so he came into the studio faithfully twice a week to study on his own. It was a way for him to rid himself of the stresses of his job. He enjoyed every moment he was dancing and this made teaching him a pleasure for Kiki.

Eventually, Edward grew tired of trying to draw more attention and the two of them left. Joan let out a sigh of relief, but it proved to be short lived. This new woman was not one who was easily swept under the rug when Edward was through with her.

A few days later as Joan was preparing the small ballroom by moving a table and chairs into the center for the staff meeting, she was once again greeted by the blond Elizabeth. Miss Tomlinson and Mr. Garrett wandered in arm in arm and sent a quick flutter of the fingers toward Joan as a greeting. Now she was a bit more concerned. Chewing slightly on her lip, she followed the two with her eyes as they entered Edward's office. Never had Edward brought someone into the studio twice. Especially not out to this studio. Once he had sufficiently shown a new conquest his empire, he no longer needed to flaunt his power around and quickly settled into showing her other things. Why was this different? Joan didn't even want to think about it.

She settled her notes for the meeting on the table in front of her chair and waited for the rest of the staff to arrive. The daily meeting started the workday of the studio. Promptly at one o'clock each afternoon, the staff would meet to go over the schedule for the day, discuss students' progress, review upcoming events, and generally motivate each other toward goals in teaching and personal dance levels. Joan thought of her job as a motivator to be one of her most crucial tasks. Maybe that was why she was so good at her job.

With Elizabeth leaning on the front reception desk, Clive Forbes took considerably longer to get to the meeting table. He almost fell all over introducing himself to the tall blond today dressed in a slim longer length belted dress with buttons all the way down the front – and a few too many at both the top and bottom unbuttoned. The khaki green color was very neutral and stylish as were her matching pumps. She wore a thin but very expensive gold necklace around her swan-like neck and gold hoops in her ears. All in all, she was simple, elegant and stylish in her attire.

Tommy and Molly entered together, both staring at Elizabeth but not saying anything as they passed her and sat down.

23

Ashley rose up to his full height when he walked in and pursing his lips in a sour lemon pout as he glanced at her without so much as a move of his head in acknowledgement. His large warm chocolate eyes were wide and truly the doorway to his soul at this moment. Elizabeth put on a plastic smile and allowed Edward to guide her toward the meeting table. She stood tall and stately with a look of dominance toward the people seated around the table. Her feet teed in a model like stance as if in a fashion show on the runway.

Edward cleared his throat and announced quite unexpectedly, "It gives me great pleasure to introduce Miss Elizabeth Tomlinson, our new counselor."

Mouths dropped open in disbelief as Miss Tomlinson put on a professional and demeaning expression. Joan Ericson's face slowly grew red with anger. And when Edward turned specifically toward Joan and announced in a flat tone that he was giving her back office to his new counselor and moving Joan to the small office overlooking the front ballroom, the smoke almost visibly rose from her ears. Her eyebrows pressed tightly together in the center, and she no longer tried to control her displeasure.

"Might I have a word with you?" Joan spoke sharply and quickly rose to lead Mr. Garrett toward her newly reassigned office. He followed.

The muffled voices could be heard behind the closed door and no one bothered to turn on the music to disguise the sounds of anger as they normally would during a "discussion" between Joan and Edward. Instead the gazes turned quickly to the tall blond who now stood with a slightly confused look on her face. Evidently she thought the news would be greeted with excitement – well, not really excitement but with cordial acceptance. They all realized she had no idea what the dance business entailed and certainly did not realize how many years of experience it normally took for a teacher to reach a management position. This was clearly an insult not only to Joan Ericson but to the rest of the people seated around this meeting table. Here was a woman who was not even a trained dancer, and she had been handed the coveted position on her merit as a "girlfriend". And a new girlfriend at that.

The tension was heavy. Kiki's steely eyes glared at Elizabeth Tomlinson who began to feel somewhat uncomfortable with the silent looks from the seated staff. The heated voices from the office behind her began to get louder and more disturbed. Finally she tossed her head and asked "What? What is the matter with you people?" Her eyes flitted from face to face expecting someone to explain the reaction. She fingered her necklace with a well manicured fingernail.

Normally a person who could empathize with a person in a difficult situation, Kiki smiled slyly. Elizabeth Tomlinson did not have her sympathies for the hole she was falling into. Kiki stood. Moving toward the stereo system, she picked out a piece of music and announced in a sugary sweet voice, "And now Miss Tomlinson will lead us all in dance session. Mambo?" The last word was pronounced with a crisp cruelty.

Kiki Mays turned abruptly toward the group as the fast Latin music began to spiral from the speakers behind her. The rest of the group quickly moved the table and chairs from the floor and stood waiting for Elizabeth Tomlinson to begin the dance session. Their stares were penetrating and hostile – all except Clive Forbes' that is. He twisted his mouth and began to mentally drink in the physical appearance of one Elizabeth Tomlinson. His hips began swaying with subtle Latin motion.

"Mambo?" Elizabeth asked sharply.

Kiki repeated the word in a strong direct voice. "Mambo! Maybe you could start with some of the Bronze styling techniques."

The circle around Elizabeth began to grow tighter as the staff surrounded her. "I'm management. Why don't you lead the …what is it…dance session?" She said with a sarcastic tone to her voice and glared right back at Kiki Mays.

Kiki smiled smugly. "Gladly." The group took partners and began to warm up with a fast Mambo. Clive grabbed Elizabeth's hand and tried to lead her through a basic Mambo step, but Elizabeth struggled. Her shoes were not dance shoes, and she stumbled awkwardly as Clive tried to be patient. His face even showed signs of frustration as he struggled to get her to even dance a basic step. He was one who could impress any partner by his patient attitude when teaching a basic pattern. That was his trick in the disco when he saw a lovely lady he wanted to take home. But this technique was not working very well on the lovely Elizabeth Tomlinson. She was stiff and hostile toward his attention. Her knees bent in an attempt to keep her balance at the fast movement, and she clung leechlike to his shoulder digging her long colorful nails into his flesh. Her feet wobbled in her high pumps, and she tried subtly to skid to a stop when Clive tried to propel her into a cross body lead and turn. They almost began to look like a pair of wrestlers fighting to desperately resisting each other's movement.

Clive's mouth began to snarl, and Elizabeth's eyes slanted into hostile take-over mode.

"How the hell do you think you are going to do the job of counselor if you can't dance? What could you – and Mr. Garrett – be thinking?" he finally spouted throwing up his hands in disgust and walking away shaking his head as Edward Garrett emerged from Joan's soon-to-be former office. Edward appeared shocked whether from the hostility of the staff toward his protégé or from the horrible display of inadequate dance ability demonstrated by Miss Tomlinson – no one quite knew which motivated his actions. He quickly grabbed Elizabeth's hand and pulled her toward the front door and out of the studio. Joan emerged from the office with a stony expression on her face and simply moved toward the table in the corner of the ballroom to continue with her meeting as planned. Everyone was silent to what just had happened. The music was turned off and chairs pushed quietly into place.

After the meeting, Kiki helped Joan put the table away and asked one question. "What are you going to do?"

"What can I do? It's Mr. Garrett's studio. All I can hope is that she totally screws up. But then, that could completely destroy the studio for good, couldn't it?" Joan sighed deeply. There were so many ways this scenario could go. Kiki nodded. Yes, it could be bad – very bad for everyone. They wanted Miss Tomlinson to fail but not at the expense of the staff and the studio. What to do?

Clive and Tommy stood silently in the back ballroom. Clive tapped his foot nervously. "I lost my cool with our Miss Lizzy," he groaned. "I thought she might be an easy one if Edward was her type."

27

Tommy grinned. "Miss Lizzy? Like the game. Struck Miss Lizzy!" His eyes glistened as he thought about that.

"What? Struck Miss Lizzy?" Clive frowned.

"Never heard of that game?" Tommy tossed a glance toward Clive. "You never played that game? The person who is 'it' comes around and picks someone saying 'struck Miss Lizzy' and that person has to hit a funny pose… Or something like that. I can't quite remember the details. It's a kids' game."

Clive shook his head and ignored the comments about a kids' game. He was focusing on the real Miss Lizzy. "I wonder what it would take…". He stopped his verbal thought process and began to internalize.

Tommy just shrugged his broad shoulders and left the ballroom. Miss Lizzy Tomlinson was not the one who peaked his interests. He glanced across the room at Molly Ross pulling out dance programs from the shelf pushed into the small ballroom's corner. She wore a long gathered skirt that was ankle length – a normal occurrence for someone on the short side – with black calfskin dance sandals peeking out beneath. Her heavy belted sweater warmed her in the early day coolness of the studio. As the day progressed, the dance floors began to heat up with the movement of dancing bodies. Molly tossed back her long mane of black hair and glanced back to notice Tommy staring at her. She smiled back.

VI.

Joan Ericson threw the empty boxes on the desk and began to toss her possessions in haphazardly. Did she really need boxes to move from one office to another, only a few feet away from each other? No. But this way if she needed to move out for good, the items would already be boxed and ready to go. It was one thing after another, wasn't it? The downtown studio moving out here into their space, the showcase to be held here in her studio, and now this Elizabeth Tomlinson character taking over her office and part of her job. It was everything that had Joan upset, worried, and angry. She had gone through this before. With Edward Garrett there was always a crisis. If it wasn't the moves from studio space to studio space, it was the staff quitting or the IRS coming in to claim back taxes. It hadn't ever been easy with Edward and the studio. There was always something to worry about. So why was this different? She just shook her head and tossed another framed photo into the box. She stared at the photo of the past staff pictured. The smiling faces looked happy. She remembered their competent abilities – now she had all these beginners. Oh, there was Kiki and of course the others were well on their way to becoming great dancers and teachers. But now she also had Elizabeth. If she helped her succeed as she knew she could, the studio would once again thrive and Joan herself would once again be in a win-win situation. But why should she help this bimbo? Why should she do the woman's job for her? To benefit the studio and these teachers – her staff? Maybe. But it was an insult and her heart was no longer into compensating for someone else. She flung a book across the room against the door with a thud. How could Edward Garrett be so infuriating? Or maybe the question was, how could he not be infuriating? She finished her packing, and Tommy showed up at her door offering to haul the boxes to the other office. Nice, nice of him, she thought with a smile.

Elizabeth Tomlinson showed up that evening at six o'clock. What? Was her day different than the rest of the staff? Joan quickly informed her that the studio began at one, and all were expected to be in attendance for the meeting and dance session with the teaching day beginning at three and lasting until ten. After all, Joan was the manager and all would follow the rules no matter who they were. Elizabeth rolled her eyes and flashed her big smile as if to indicate that she would be coming and going as she pleased. Then Miss Lizzy went into her office and closed the door sharply. Joan frowned. This was not going to be an easy task – saving this studio from that woman. Not an easy task at all.

Edward was in the studio as well and managed to find his way to Elizabeth's office for about an hour. Then he guided her into Joan's office – the door was always opened unless she was meeting with a student – and indicated Elizabeth should sit down in the chair in front of Joan's desk.

"Miss Ericson, could you please explain to Miss Tomlinson what her job and duties entail?" Edward clearly was realizing he had gotten himself into a sticky situation. He was washing his hands of training this new hire, even if she was his girlfriend. His mind had shifted to the running of the studio, and the image was not developing into a pleasant picture.

Joan Ericson smiled. "Gladly! I'll just get the appointment sheets and go over her schedule." She abruptly rose and walked slowly toward the front desk leaving the two of them seated in her office glaring at each other. Let them sit and stew for a while she decided. She would be in no hurry to return.

She took her time paging through the large appointment sheets normally clipped to a board on the top of the front desk. The top row of the sheet was for the new student department. Joan would have to cross off her name on the left side in the counselor column and replace it with Elizabeth's. The new student teachers were listed across the top of the page. Normally Tommy, Molly, and Ashley took the new students until they were ready to move to an advanced teacher. The lower half of the schedule was devoted to the advanced department. Joan's name in the left column would remain intact. She was still the supervisor and would continue to head the advanced department along with her advanced teachers Clive, Kiki and occasionally Ashley. She picked up a number two pencil along with a two-tipped blue and red one. She grabbed the card catalogue with the student cards and sauntered back to her new office.

Joan's desk was still clean and clear, so she plunked down the large sheets and flipped them around so Elizabeth could see the writing. Elizabeth Tomlinson pressed her back into the chair and crossed her arms belligerently with a scowl on her face as Joan picked up the pencil and pointed to the column on the top left of the page. Joan put a crisp cross through the name "Ericson" and penciled in "Tomlinson".

"This is your column with your appointments. When an interview comes in we schedule that student with a teacher, either Tommy McLaughlin or Molly Ross and then with you. The appointment is written in pencil with an indication to the left above the new student's name in red. The name will be written in blue in your column as well. You do the initial interview and then take the student out to the front ballroom for their lesson with the teacher. You got that so far?" Joan stared at Elizabeth's face – stony and cold. "Maybe you should take notes," she suggested pushing a pad and pen over in Elizabeth's direction. They both went untouched. Joan continued. "When the lesson is over, you take the student into your office and present the program options available to continue with lessons." Joan pulled out a sheet of paper from her top desk draw. "These are the three programs we offer to new students. Each includes private lessons, group lessons, and our practice party sessions." Elizabeth craned her neck and finally uncrossed her arms to lean forward glancing at the paper Joan had turned in front of her to review. "Here take it and look it over. Prices along with new student discounts are listed along the side of each program." She shoved the paper to the front of the desk and waited for Elizabeth to slowly inch her hand forward toward the paper. "This is your bread and butter, so I'd know this information inside and out if I were you."

Joan clasped her hands on the top of the desk and waited. Elizabeth's eyes bugged slightly as she reviewed the sheet. The prices for each course were indeed printed along the right side of the sheet. Joan leaned over and put a line through each of the prices. "If the student enrolls in a program that evening, we offer them a discounted price. So these prices become these prices…". Joan scribbled in the new prices in pencil along the side of the ink printed number. Elizabeth twisted her mouth.

It took a few minutes for Elizabeth to even comprehend anything that was explained to her. "I would suggest you take a good look at these programs and these prices because your first interview will be tonight. And another suggestion," Joan paused waiting for Elizabeth to raise her eyes to meet Joan's glare. "I would strongly suggest you figure out how to dance. It doesn't bow well with our teachers or our students if the counselor doesn't have a clue about our product." Their locked stares remained steady for a few seconds until Elizabeth looked down – she lost the staring contest this time. She picked up the course sheet glanced back at the schedule still spread out neatly on the top of Joan's desk and walked stiffly out of the office. Edward remained slumped in his chair. He hadn't said a word through the entire explanation. Now he sat staring at the back wall.

Joan rose and grabbed the appointment sheets to return to the desk. "Don't you have your own office?" she asked curtly as she left to cross the dance floor to the reception desk. Edward sighed and returned to his office. She imagined he was asking himself what he was doing as he sat in his dark office with the door closed.

Joan actually enjoyed the rest of the day – there was no sound from either of the offices. Edward must be brooding because he was nowhere to be seen, and Elizabeth was hopefully studying her material in her own office with the curtains closed. As the teaching evening started Joan watched carefully for the new student scheduled for seven o'clock. Would Elizabeth show at the front desk for the interview? Joan stayed close to the front of the studio waiting.

"Mr. Brant?" Joan greeted the bewildered looking middle aged man who wandered in a few minutes before seven. "Please fill out this information sheet for me, and the counselor will be with you in just a moment." She smiled sweetly trying to make the nervous man feel comfortable. He smiled and sat down on one of the sofas in the reception area and studied the sheet Joan had handed him. When no one emerged from Elizabeth's office, Joan sighed and approached the man again.

"Thanks for completing this questionnaire. Why don't you follow me to my office and we'll get you started." Joan took his elbow and as they passed through the small ballroom Joan gave a scenic tour of the studio. "And over here is the board announcing our upcoming events…". He began to relax a bit as he looked the events board over carefully noticing all of the smiling faces of the students and staff dancing and flashing confident grins into the camera.

After Joan reviewed Mr. Brant's reasons for learning to dance and what situations he could visualize himself using social dancing, she went over the list of the most popular dances. They selected a few that might work for what Mr. Brant needed. His face lit up as Joan described each dance in more detail. The words she used were "socially confident" and "popular partner". Mr. Brant seemed pleased. Then Joan rose and escorted Mr. Brant out to the small ballroom to meet Miss Ross.

As the two emerged from Joan's office, Elizabeth Tomlinson stood in her doorway. Her face appeared blank as her eyes followed the two out to the floor. Later, thought Joan. I will deal with her later.

"Miss Ross, let me introduce you to Mr. Brant…" Joan reviewed the dances they had just discussed. Molly smiled and immediately made her student feel at ease with a soothing chuckle. Joan left the two to begin their lesson. She swung by Elizabeth's doorway and hissed under her breath, "That was your student. Where were you?"

Elizabeth looked surprised at Joan's comment then scowled. "Did you forget the lesson scheduled for seven? Check your schedule, please. If you need me to cover your students, the least you could do is observe so you know the procedures." Then Joan turned and reentered her office leaving the door open to keep an eye on the progress of the lesson.

In about twenty minutes, Joan reemerged and looked around for Elizabeth. Again, she was nowhere to be found. She shook her head slowly and descended upon Molly and Mr. Brant. "How is he doing?" she asked cheerfully, her dimples accenting her cheeks.

Molly glowed as she described what they had covered, and they demonstrated a near perfect Fox Trot. Joan nodded and watched the Waltz and then a basic Swing step. Joan thanked Molly and led Mr. Brant back into her office to review his progress in more detail and show him the possibilities for furthering his dancing. She felt confident Mr. Brant would decide to continue. His lesson had gone very well in spite of the no show from Elizabeth Tomlinson. And indeed he did. He selected the middle program and signed on the dotted line. Joan took him back up to the front desk and arranged for the receptionist to schedule his next few lessons with Molly. "Please make sure you schedule Miss Tomlinson to review his progress on his fourth lesson," Joan smiled as she listed her instructions. Then she handed Mr. Brant the schedule for the weekly groups and practice session. She circled the groups she would recommend for a beginning student.

He studied the paper carefully with a not-so-nervous any more smile.

Normally Joan Ericson walked with short relaxed steps, but at that moment her steps were crisp and quick. She moved right to Elizabeth's door and knocked loudly. Without waiting for an answer, she opened the door and walked in. Elizabeth was seated with her legs splayed knees pressed together and her eyes half closed. She was comfortably leaning back in her overstuffed office chair – the one Joan had enjoyed for so long prior to Elizabeth Tomlinson's arrival.

Joan pursed her lips together and began tapping on the top of the desk. "So, my dear, where were you? Your student just bought lessons. But you, unfortunately, were nowhere to be seen. That, again unfortunately, is your job. So if you ever miss a new student lesson again, you'll be fired. Understand?"

This exchange opened Elizabeth's eyes and with a smart grin on her face shook her head. "You can't do that, I'm afraid. I own this position and there is nothing you can do about it." She grinned again.

"Oh, really? We'll just see about that." Joan turned to leave and then wheeled back smartly to add "and by the way, your paycheck is based on your sales. So at the moment you have zero dollars earned." Joan marched down to Edward Garrett's office.

She knocked on Edward's door and again didn't wait for an answer. "Edward? I need a few words with you, please."

VII.

Edward stood in his tenth floor condo gazing out the window at the sprinkle of lights across the downtown city area. He loved this sight. His mind began to wander back to the events of the day. He knew Joan Ericson was right about Elizabeth. She had no idea what the dance business was about and was nowhere near qualified for the position he had given her. At the time, it seemed so perfect. It was a matter of impressing a beautiful woman – a young beautiful woman. But as he now considered his finances, the idea looked to be rather foolish. He brooded about what to do next. Money or the woman? Which one would win the battle in his head?

"Daddy," Elizabeth called from the doorway to the bedroom. She leaned against the frame wearing next to nothing and looked every inch the model she was. Her chin tilted down in a little girl pout letting her yellow hair stream across her face.

"I told you never to call me that name," he hissed before turning to face her. When he saw her blond bang sweeping across her cheek and the soft pale color of her smooth skin, he recanted. How could he say anything in that tone to someone so beautiful? He sighed and tilted his head back to gaze at her body. Not what he was used to! He had always been drawn to tall anorexic looking bony models with flat chests and here was a woman with round breasts, a tiny waist and curving hips above long toned legs. She had no protruding sharpness. Instead she looked like a beautiful angel. His lips curled into a bowed smile.

"OK," she said lowering her chin even more and widening her eyes in a sorry puppy-dog expression. "Come in here." She extended a hand beckoning him with an outstretched finger to follow her. He couldn't help himself and retreated into the bedroom watching her saunter in ahead of him with her smooth pale bottom swaying suggestively from side to side.

"That Joan Ericson is just horrible," Elizabeth whined in a little girl voice as she lay on the plush bed inviting him to join her. "Why do you let her run that studio – your studio?"

Edward collapsed on the bed and began explaining, "Miss Ericson is a very talented woman, and the studio needs someone with her abilities to keep running smoothly." But his voice trailed off as Elizabeth began to run her finger up and down his body.

"I suppose, but you are the genius behind the whole business." She continued to walk her fingers up and down as Edward lay back with his eyes closed. "You deserve the credit for everything successful about that studio." She let her words sink in and then continued. "I think you deserve much more attention and recognition than you receive from your staff – and from other dancers all across the country. I can imagine what people would say if they saw you not only dancing and choreographing but with a beautiful woman on your arm to show them how successful you are in your personal life as well."

Edward was slowly feeling himself drawn into Elizabeth's glowing picture. She continued to outline her plan. "I understand the studio is sponsoring a dance event…".

"The Showcase," Edward Garrett corrected.

"Will there be important people attending?" Elizabeth leaned back watching Edward's eyes caress her body.

"Our judges will be Glen and Elena Kelly, the current ten dance champions who have been the premier names in the dance world throughout the United States for the past decade. They are certainly very important dancers – maybe the most important people presently." Edward continued to stare at Elizabeth longingly. He licked his lips.

"What would they say if you walked in with a beautiful woman on your arm?" She grinned seductively as she slid the strap to her near see through negligee off one shoulder.

"And who would that beautiful woman be?" he asked teasingly with a slight shake of his head. She gave him a playful slap on his shoulder but giggled back. "I think if we ..." and she outlined her idea even further.

Back in the studio, Joan Ericson was finishing up her paperwork. She listed all of the new students and recorded the number of lessons purchased this week by both the new student and the advanced department. "Hopefully, by tomorrow I will be back doing both jobs again," she sighed to herself as she carefully recorded the numbers into her weekly report. She had made her position perfectly clear, and Edward Garrett seemed to listen. He knew she was right – Elizabeth Tomlinson was certainly not the right person for the position of counselor. She wasn't even right for any staff position if Joan had anything to say about it. The question now was where were Edward's priorities? Would he choose the success of the studio or the success of his personal sex life? She sighed. When she put it that way, she had the horrible feeling she was losing the battle. Would that dreadful Elizabeth Tomlinson walk in again tomorrow? She would wait and see.

Yes. Elizabeth did walk in – Joan had indeed failed in her quest to save the integrity of the studio. Not only did Elizabeth walk in the next day, but she was late. She showed up half way through the meeting and headed straight for her office, not even bothering to join the staff as they went over the daily schedule. Joan hoped no one had a camera because her look at Elizabeth as she sauntered by the meeting table could have killed.

Edward Garrett followed moving across the floor and standing confidently in front of the group. Without so much as a notice of what material Joan was presenting, he began to speak. "I would like to discuss the upcoming Showcase," he began. Joan glared but tried to calm down quickly. Take a deep breath she told herself. She was interested in what he was planning to do – after all, she would be the one carrying out the plans for the Showcase.

"We are going to hold the event here in the studio." He smiled as if he had just said something funny. "We have been contacted by the state regarding the issue of requiring staff to attend events without pay. Although I view you all as independent contractors who should be using every advantage to service your customers – your students, the government doesn't see it that way. So we will pay each of you for the performances you dance with your students at the Showcase, but the dance following the competition will be an unpaid event. Therefore, if you choose not to attend, that is your business. But I would strongly recommend you stay and service your students as a way to build your business and therefore, your income." He smiled broadly after this statement and noticed Joan Ericson nodding in agreement. The staff looked at each other with confused looks on their faces. They were trying to comprehend what he was referring to. Maybe this was an issue that created the past staff to quit….hmmm.

"Now onto the details of the event." Edward described the dance couple, the Kellys who would be judging the event and performing at the dance after the competition. His comments about their expertise were glowing. His hope was to build the excitement for his novice staff and increase his own income. Edward was shrewd as he pumped up his staff. Joan knew this was his forte, and she hoped they would listen. He described the intent of having students participate in a Showcase and scheduling times the next day with the judges for comments and suggestions on future dance goals. Joan had to admit, Edward Garrett was at his finest. She could feel the excitement building as he spoke. Hopefully, the enthusiasm would continue not only for the rest of the day, but for the rest of the week until the event was held.

After the meeting, Joan pulled Clive and Tommy aside and asked if they would help selecting and playing music at the Showcase. She wanted to get them involved and to teach them more about finding a suitable tempo for each of the dances. This could be a great educational experience.

"Could you stay after hours tonight and select some music you feel appropriate so I can check through it tomorrow?" she asked.

Clive sighed. "Well, I have plans… but I suppose I could stay for a bit if Tom is agreeable." He turned to Tommy who was nodding. Yes, he was willing to stay as well.

The studio was almost empty. The teaching day was over with the rest of the staff gone home, and Clive and Tommy had stacks of music selected in piles on the back table. Clive would play a little piece, and they would try a few patterns to see how the tempo felt and which dance was most appropriate. Clive liked music, and he was actually enjoying himself as the beat pounded loudly across the large back ballroom. He had a great knowledge of what was currently popular with his nightly outings to the city's hot spots. "Listen to this one," he exclaimed as he began to move around the floor and pound with his body to the background beat of the music. His lean tall body had a natural fluid expression.

The curtains to the office Elizabeth Tomlinson occupied opened slightly. She peered out at the two men as they danced. After a few minutes, she opened the curtains fully and stood staring out with the light in the background silhouetting her body. Slowly she began to unbutton her top carefully making sure Clive noticed as he spun closer and closer to the window. His head turned, and he stopped dancing as she unbuttoned lower and lower almost to the bottom of her short dress. She smiled and gestured for the two of them to come into her office. They looked at each other and without a spoken word between the two moved to the door of the office. Clive opened the door, and the two entered.

Elizabeth was almost completely undressed by the time the two entered. Standing behind the desk, she leaned forward, opened her desk drawer and pulled out an ornately cut glass bottle of golden liquor. She raised the bottle as if to offer the liquid to the two. Clive didn't drink and his eyebrow rose slightly. Tommy just shook his head and whispered, "Not my poison, thanks."

Elizabeth licked her lips and began to take a swig. Then putting the bottle on her desk began to reach around to unfasten her bra. Tommy elbowed Clive, and Clive looked back at Tommy.

42

Tommy knew what Clive was thinking – this was a rare opportunity. It was also something that could destroy both their careers in this studio especially when it came to crossing Edward Garrett. The wheels were turning in both their heads. What would they do? Suddenly, Tommy turned and walked out the door and headed toward the front door of the studio. Not worth it, he thought. Clive followed but with hesitation looking back to catch a few more glimpses of the woman who continued her striptease. He wasn't quite as sure of this decision, but didn't want to be the one caught.

As they walked out the door, the naked Elizabeth Tomlinson stood in her doorway and called after them, "Chickens!" Her words began to slur and elongate as she repeated it several times more.

"Not a word of this to anyone," Clive hissed. "I have my reputation, you know."

"My lips are sealed," Tommy replied back as he jumped into his black car and roared off across the parking lot.

They would have to come up with an excuse in the morning for leaving the stacks of music still on the table in the back ballroom. But that would be easier than the alternative.

VIII.

The studio began to take on a new life. Joan had the staff decorate the studio with subtle yet creative beauty. There were garlands of flowers and an archway strung between the reception area and the small ballroom where the buffet table would be. Joan selected a menu that would be elegant yet easy. Normally, the guests in a Showcase would enjoy a dinner at a hotel before the evening dance. But this would have to change with the studio hosting the event. The meal would have to be something simple to serve yet beautiful in appearance. Joan chose a fruit salad cut into a watermelon half for color. There would be vegetable platters with dips, cheese and meat plates, crackers, and of course desserts. Cut candy dishes filled with silver and gold wrapped chocolates, an array of cookies and bars and slices of cheesecake drizzled with strawberries and chocolate. Joan had asked Megan Meeker, the manager of the downtown studio to select several trainees to serve food and punch. They were on duty dressed in elegant black – dresses for the ladies and tuxes for the gentlemen.

Clive and Tommy had finished arranging the music for the dance competition. They had surprised her with a good selection. She had showered the two with praise but they seemed surprisingly humble. "Humble". That was certainly not a word she had ever imagined using to describe Clive Forbes, but he genuinely seemed suited to that word when she complimented him on the music task.

Kiki Mays was excited. She would be performing with several of her students, and she was ready. The dances chosen and choreographed had worked out perfectly. She had a gift for showmanship and putting together just the right movements for a showstopper performance. That was something she had always felt even during times of self doubt. Meeting Glen and Elena Kelly was something else she was looking forward to. It should be an amazing experience. She intended to enjoy every moment of that day. She had spent the morning arranging her several dresses for the performances in a small room set aside to store costumes. The blue one was spectacular, and the cream skirt flowed with elegance. Kiki fingered each sleek dress hanging on their hangers to make sure all of the stonework and lace was properly attached. With a shake of the garment, she fingered the soft feel of the fabrics in anticipation.

Glen and Elena walked into the studio along with Edward Garrett. Elizabeth was gripping Edward's arm. Glen and Elena looked the perfect couple – both tiny and dark haired – they suited each other as dancers and as husband and wife. Glen was athletic in build wearing a black tuxedo and outgoing smile. Elena was small and slender with her glistening black hair wrapped into a French twist. Her smart black suit was accented with a red satin blouse and a simple gold chain around her neck. In comparison Elizabeth looked tall – almost giant. She seemed to slouch forward when she spoke to the two. There was almost a hesitation to her manner today that was unusual. Elizabeth was dressed in a simple pale blue dress that was a bit too summery for the occasion but as always it was crisp and elegant.

Edward gave them the grand tour. Joan was seated in her office with the door opened and stood to greet the two with a kiss on the cheek. Elizabeth's eyes glared at their familiarity. The Kellys seemed to know Joan almost better than they knew Edward. Joan joked and laughed with the two on their travel woes – would their bags arrive on time, etc. She asked about their children and their dogs. What didn't she know about the Kellys?

"And which hotel did Edward book for you?" she asked cheerfully.

"We are staying at Hotel Garrett," they pleasantly announced with a chuckle.

"What?" Joan looked confused. "Do we have a Hotel Garrett in Minneapolis?"

"We thought it would be more intimate for them to stay at my condo with Elizabeth and myself," Edward smiled at the Kellys, and they smiled back at him.

"Yes, it's lovely," Elena commented with a guarded tone to her voice but the businesslike smile on her face still present. "The view is amazing." She nodded. "We could see the entire city from way up there." Her voice dragged a bit on the "way up there" part of her sentence.

"Well, good," Joan nodded trying to stay upbeat when she was really thinking how cheap Edward was. "Let me show you the scoring sheets and the schedule." She led the two into the back ballroom and pointed out the judge's table. "Students and staff should be coming in soon."

The small talk continued. Elizabeth and Edward stood back away from the group, Elizabeth trying to keep a smile on her face and digging her fingernails into Edward's arm. Was she reassuring enough? She hoped so.

The room began to fill with people all laughing and chatting. Some of the downtown staff ambled in as if to size up the room and imagine being here in the future. They pointed out things in the room and nodded. Would they enjoy moving out here for a while? The staff office was certainly going to be cramped.

Carrying garment bags over their arms, they moved on to the small room reserved for costumes.

As the event was to begin, Edward Garrett stood by the microphone to welcome the guests and introduce the judges. He brought Glen and Elena to the front, introducing them with glowing remarks about their accomplishments and dance titles. Glen spoke a bit excited by the opportunity to be here to work with the "wonderful staff and students from Minneapolis". He was perfect and cordial in his remarks heightening the excitement to dance for him and receive helpful comments to improve. It was just as expected – the typical speeches until Edward took back the microphone for a closing remark.

"I would also like to introduce someone else very special," he reached for Elizabeth Tomlinson's hand. "This is Elizabeth Tomlinson our new counselor in this studio." There was a cordial amount of clapping. Then he continued. "Miss Tomlinson is not only going to be our counselor, but she will also take on a new title." Joan Ericson gasped – her face turning from stony nonreactive to seething anger in anticipation of what was to come. Edward continued, "She will soon be Mrs. Edward Garrett." The whole audience was silent for a moment and then the clapping was begun by one of the students who had never met Elizabeth Tomlinson before. Slowly the rest of the room joined in until a steady monotonous pounding sounded. Joan Ericson gasped again. She had been beaten. Lost. Defeated. Elizabeth Tomlinson held up a hand displaying a sparkling diamond ring with a gigantic stone. Glen and Elena Kelly moved in to congratulate the couple and compliment the lovely sparkler. Edward Garrett's face was puffed with pride.

The dance staff scrambled to get things moving after the surprising announcement. The first dance was just a simple warm up Fox Trot for all who were competing as well as those who were there for the show. The space became crowded, and Joan scurried around putting up additional chairs in the corners and along the walls for the visitors. No time to worry about Edward's latest disaster. She moved up toward Edward still at the microphone and tactfully suggested he read the list of the first group of dancers so they could leave the room to line up in the small ballroom. There was a second dance so those competing could prepare. Those watching the show were invited to Waltz while they waited for the first performance.

Kiki Mays dressed in a sparkling pink dress with a floating skirt stood in the doorway with her student Mr. Nelson for the first number, another Waltz. Mr. Nelson was a tad bit shorter than Kiki as she stood in her heel. They smiled at each other and proceeded out to the center of the floor when Edward announced their names. Elena and Glen were seated at the judges' table across the floor next to the sound system. They smiled at the couple and nodded inviting them to begin with the music. A lovely instrumental Waltz began to play, and Kiki stretched out to the side and swirled around Mr. Nelson in an elegant introduction. Then the couple began to dance around the floor smoothly incorporating a soothing rise and fall motion. They moved from twinkle to spiral and then into a series of pivots. Mr. Nelson's footwork brought nods from the judges who began to furiously write on their note pads as he moved around the corner and turned Kiki into an elegant underarm turn. She stretched out into a sweeping line smiling at the seated audience. Mr. Nelson swept her back into his arms and into a long low dip. The claps were loud and long for a beautiful first performance. Kiki smiled broadly as she led Mr. Nelson from the floor. The second couple moved out to the middle of the floor with nervous anticipation.

The Showcase continued on with couple after couple dancing a variety of dances from Waltz to Fox Trot to Tango and Latin dances. Kiki and Mr. Nelson danced another performance in the middle of the show – a fast crisp Cha Cha. Dressed in a sleek brilliant blue dress with lines of glitter and a sparkling pair of gold Latin sandals, Kiki's costume brought loud applause from the crowd. Their dancing brought even more approval. They were clearly a favorite couple. Clive smiled proudly as he clicked the music to the next piece. Kiki Mays was an amazing dancer to watch. Smooth and elegant yet rhythmic and precise – she was eye catching. Her face showed no signs of nervousness, instead she displayed a real connection with the crowd with every expression.

When the competition itself was complete, Edward invited the guests to enjoy the buffet table and take a break while the judges tabulated scores. The room cleared out a bit, and Clive put on gentle piece of background music. Elizabeth worked the room, moving around to the groups who remained to introduce herself. Megan Meeker, the manager of the downtown studio walked over to meet the new executive. Megan was always a unique person in appearance. Tonight she had on a bright red flowing dress that accented her short cropped hair with hunks of red streaks in the bangs. She wore a chunky gold necklace and matching earrings. Her red lips were as always full and glossy.

"I understand we will be sharing office space soon," she began when she caught Elizabeth's attention.

In her smoky voice, Elizabeth sounded confused. "What? Huh, you are…?" Elizabeth leaned forward waiting for an answer from the stunning woman standing in front of her with a wide grin on her face.

"Oh, excuse me. I'm Megan Meeker, the manager of the downtown studio." Megan extended her hand with glistening red nails studded with tiny gems. Elizabeth frowned but shook the hand.

"You do know the downtown studio is going to be using this space for a few months until our new downtown location is ready, don't you?" Megan continued with her explanation sensing a lack of connection from Elizabeth.

Again Elizabeth frowned. "And I'm Anna Smith, the downtown supervisor," another woman joined in. Anna Smith was actually younger than she appeared. She had a matronly appearance with short curls that haloed her pleasant face. She was dressed nicely in a forest green skirt and ruffled blouse. Slightly taller than Megan, Anna was a stunning dancer with a most un-model like figure. At this moment, Elizabeth seemed totally unaware there even was a downtown studio. And she seemed even more shocked there existed a whole new group of executives to contend with. She blinked her eyes rapidly and stared at the two new faces. "Oh, my," was all she could manage to get out.

Edward spotted the three of them and took long strides across the ballroom to reach the group. "Miss Smith… and Miss Meeker. How nice to see you both. You haven't met my lovely fiancé have you?" Edward was his energetic self putting his arm around Elizabeth's shoulder.

Elizabeth glared at him and shook off his arm. "Counselor as well," she added to his introduction. "I am the counselor of this studio." Her smile plastered thinly across her peach toned face as she leaned closer to them with this quick announcement.

"As am I," Megan smiled cheerfully. "And I am the manager as well." Megan's voice crept higher in tone as she added the last part. "I've been with Mr. Garrett here for, oh, six or seven years. Depends on how you count it. I was a student first. So I had a good foundation in my dancing before moving into the ranks of staff."

Ignoring the whole conversation and the tone of the voices, Edward continued. "And are you lovely ladies looking forward to joining the staff out here in a week or two?" He looked again from face to face with a cheeky plastered on smile. His hands rubbed together waiting for their answers.

"Well, it certainly will be tight," Megan commented looking around the room twisting her mouth into a grimace. "I guess I hadn't noticed how small the space is – compared to the place we have now of course. I suppose nothing can compare to the space we have now."

"Those offices will get a little crowded when we all fight for our interview space," Anna added pointing to the two offices now occupied by Joan and Elizabeth.

"Yeah, we'll have to get a system down, won't we?" Megan grinned at Elizabeth. "When I have my new students, I'll get the office and when you have your interviews, you'll get it. Share and share alike." Elizabeth frowned and glared again at Edward who had now turned his head to pay attention to Anna.

"You two will just love the space in the new center when we get moved in. The space is small, but so elegant. The time out here will be worth it. But we'll have to figure out a way to divide up the students by location so you keep the students you teach out here. It's got to be more convenient for them downtown, or they'll want to stay here…". Edward continued a flowing conversation about the new studio space to appease his two downtown executives. All the while, Elizabeth was becoming more and more irritated. Her face began to distort into an ugly expression. She was no longer the beauty she was when she walked into the room with a sparkling diamond on her finger and a vision of admiration from the dance crowd. Her dream day was quickly fading minute by minute.

As if by miracle, the Kellys snatched up the microphone and invited the crowd to rejoin them for the results. The people with plates of food and cups of punch ambled back into the large ballroom to retake their seats. Snippets of conversation rose and fell. Elizabeth quickly moved Edward away from Megan and Anna to retreat to a corner for a discussion.

"You never told me…", she hissed as she pulled him toward the restroom area. Their voices were muffled and angry as Glen Kelly valiantly tried to list the awards in a louder voice than theirs. He smiled patiently and hoped someone – anyone – would quiet the din from the back hallway. But no one ventured toward the area occupied by Edward Garrett and his future bride.

Kiki Mays and her student Mr. Nelson won the top award in the advanced division. Each student was placed in a category according to their ability level – beginner, intermediate, and advanced. Although Mr. Nelson was the hands down favorite of the crowd, Molly Ross and her beginning student Allan Spencer easily won the praise of both audience and judges with their country western two-step. Wearing cowboy boots and western shirts, they danced around the floor to a new and popular country song that had the crowd clapping their hands and whistling. When Glen Kelly announced they had taken the top honors in the beginning level, the audience showed their approval with loud hoots and stomps on the floor. The noise drowned out the continuing argument of Elizabeth and Edward Garrett. Glen and Elena Kelly relaxed a bit as the guests began to get into the spirit of the Showcase and showed their enthusiastic approval every time he announced a name and an award.

Finally, when all awards were presented, and still no sign of Edward Garrett, Glen looked around frantically for Joan to take over the microphone. She made it to the front of the ballroom and relieved the poor judge from trying to entertain the audience. "We will take an hour break before beginning the evening dance where you may practice your own steps with other students and staff members. In addition, our judges, Elena and Glen Kelly will present an amazing show. They are truly the top dancers in the United States if not in the world. It is a show you will not want to miss!" Her face glowed with anticipation. She was rewarded with a round of applause from those crowding the room. The two judges bowed slightly toward the audience.

"Well, I'm out of here," Clive Forbes announced to Tommy as they rearranged the music selections. He leaned on the shelf holding the sound equipment, his gangly legs and arms crossing in a relaxed yet defiant position. He sneered and nodded his head toward the doorway.

"What do you mean?" Tommy's eyebrows furrowed as he quickly glanced over at Clive.

"Didn't you hear what Edward said the other day in meeting? We are not required to stay for the dance because they aren't paying us." Clive pulled up to his full height and gave Tommy a sly smile. "I'm going out to the clubs and dance with some beautiful babes – not these middle aged biddies. I'm gonna see if I can hook up with Donnette Hubble at that new club downtown – the one with the larger dance floor. She frequents that place, I think. You with me bro?"

Tommy looked around at the students milling around. They were certainly not young and chic like the club scene offered. "You can't socialize with a student. That's against the studio policy," Tommy whispered, his eyes down.

"So? Who's going to know? Everyone else will be here. You with me or not?" Clive demanded nervously tapping his foot.

"Yeah. I guess so," Tommy dragged out reluctantly. "Let me get my things."

He headed toward the teachers' office passing Molly Ross who was accepting congratulations with her cowboy student. She smiled as Tommy walked by, excused herself to follow him into the office to find out what was happening. He clearly looked frustrated and agitated by something.

"Clive and I are leaving," Tommy announced when Molly asked him why he was taking his dance shoes off. "We're going downtown to the clubs. After all, Edward said staff didn't have to stay for the dance, remember? They aren't paying us. Why don't you come along?"

"Are you stupid or something," Molly frowned. "These students are your job, your money, your paycheck. How idiotic is it to walk out with Clive Forbes? How important is this job to you? I've worked too hard to do something like that." Molly was clearly angry. She shook her head and stared at his turning head. He stared at her short body with folded arms across her ample chest.

Tommy took a deep breath. He felt caught. Both had good arguments, and he felt torn between the two. "Listen, I'm going to the clubs, but I'll be back for you after the dance is over," he promised.

"Right. I'm afraid once you leave, you won't make it back. Have fun!" And with that, Molly turned and stomped out of the office back to the dance floor. She grabbed Kiki and pulled her to a back corner. "Clive and Tommy are taking off," she announced.

"What do you mean?" Kiki's eyes narrowed. Her lips pressed together into a tight line.

"When Mr. Garrett said the staff was not going to be paid for the dance part of the Showcase and would not be required to stay, those two decided it would be more fun to go downtown dancing at the clubs," Molly's voice was irritated. "Tommy said he would come back after the dance was over, but I doubt that will happen..." She realized she had said too much and let her voice trail off.

55

"What is going on with you two? Aren't you married?" Kiki demanded but then let her mind move on to the problem with Clive. "How can he not realize how important it is to service students? So now you and I are left to take care of our clients. That really makes me angry. Where is he?" She began to look around the room. "I suppose they've already slipped out. The weasels." She put her hands on her hips and surveyed the group milling around waiting for the dance to begin. "They are going to miss out big time." Kiki spotted Joan Ericson chatting with Anna and Megan. She swiftly glided across the floor to tell Joan of the latest developments with her staff. Molly tried to make herself small and avoid answering any questions about the Showcase situation or about Tommy.

Joan and Kiki moved to a back corner for a private conversation. Megan leaned over and whispered to Anna. "So how much of our studio profit went toward that huge diamond ring on Miss Fiancé's finger? I'm betting a lot!" she mumbled. "No wonder we have to move out of our space and move to a smaller studio. Oh, yes. I forgot about our little vacation out here with Miss prissy while we wait." Megan, usually a cheerful addition to any conversation, was not the life of the party any more.

Anna nodded. "No wonder we can never make ends meet. We work and work for his highness to spend it all on someone like her." She flipped her curly top toward the back restroom area where Elizabeth and Edward were still in the midst of their argument. Anna never felt a kinship toward any of Edward's model companions. Elizabeth was no exception. In fact Elizabeth was the worst of all – she actually managed to get him to buy her a

56

diamond and announce their engagement. How had she arranged that one?

The dance began with the lights dimmed and the music playing. A traditional Fox Trot was the first dance selection and the couples quickly filled the floor to try some promenades and twinkles. Kiki asked Mr. Nelson to dance. He was all smiles with his success in the competition. The music playing made Kiki relax a bit and enjoy the event. She looked forward to the upcoming show. The Kellys had an impeccable reputation. Kiki and Mr. Nelson discussed the lesson they would take in the beginning of the week with the couple and decided on some questions they would ask the pair.

The attendees were not disappointed. After about forty-five minutes and a few more dances for the students and guests, Glen and Elena Kelly emerged. Glen wore a simple tailored black tux, but Elena's dress was incredible. It was a mixture of silver and black perfectly fit to Elena's tiny figure. The glitter of the stonework was eye catching, and the skirt flowed with a sweep across the floor that created gasps from the women in the crowd who were thrilled with the elegance of its movement. The two began with a show tune – a Fox Trot – and moved immediately after into an elegant Waltz. Then quickly they moved to a fast Viennese Waltz with small but gliding steps across the floor pressing the crowd back into the wall to give the couple full access to the dance floor. Then after a gracious thank you from Joan to give them a quick break, the two danced a sultry Tango with dips, flares and some dynamic lifts to wow the audience. Finally, they ended with a Quickstep – a dance with fast and furious footwork and running patterns across the floor from corner to corner. The crowd erupted in applause as the Kellys bowed and ran off the floor with a wave to the crowd.

"Glen and Elena will be back in a few minutes to present their Latin show," Joan announced putting on a Tango for the crowd to try. Once again the floor filled with dancers eager to try some of the movements they saw from the performances. There was a mild din of chatter from the dancers discussing the show they had just witnessed. After another half hour, they were instructed to take their seats for the conclusion of the show. They eagerly sat as Glen and Elena Kelly once again moved out to the center of the floor.

Glen wore a black jumpsuit that allowed him more freedom of movement and accentuated his muscular physique. He tensely waited for Elena who spun out to the floor wearing a long black cape that covered her from head to toe. Suddenly she swept the cape from her shoulders and tossed it across the room to Joan who was waiting to catch the garment. Elena was wearing a skin tight Latin dress with flesh colored sleeves and bodice giving the appearance of nudity. Her breasts and hips were covered with panels of yellow glitter and floating layers of ruffles from her backside that swished as she swiveled her hips. Her Latin sandals were flesh tone making her short legs look miles long. With her suntanned body and black hair now floating behind her in a twisted ponytail, the canary yellow color popped.

They began with a quick Cha Cha featuring fast moving footwork and the shaking hips typical of a Latin dance. Then they moved into a slow romantic Rumba that brought oohs and aahs from the crowd. The two clung together and moved from lift to swirling drop leaving the viewers wondering how their bodies could move so smoothly together. Next, they moved to a bouncing Samba – the dance from Brazil – and then to a fast Mambo. Again Joan gave the two a breather as she announced they would be dancing a Jive and then a Bolero. She also thanked the two for an extraordinary show and reminded the students to sign up for coaching lessons with the pair beginning Monday. Then Elena and Glen danced a fast and furious Jive with lots of kicks and spins – a crowd pleasing performance. Finally, they danced a slow Bolero with a heart stopping rise and fall movement bringing the two together and then apart into crisp and dramatic lines. The audience was on its feet clapping enthusiastically when the show ended and the Kellys bowed again and again accepting the praise of the viewers. When the clapping died down, the students eagerly began to race for the front reception desk to make appointments with the pair. Kiki and Molly grinned at each other and sighed. What an incredible experience and so encouraging for a teacher and dancer. Ashley was beside himself with enthusiasm. He gushed his praises to Kiki and Molly and then on to Joan. The dance was over on this incredible high note. The air tingled with enthusiasm.

The staff from both studios formed their usual reception line to send off the students and guests in a timely manner. Soon the ballroom was cleared and quickly cleaned. The trainees from the downtown had already packed up the food and taken down the tables from the buffet area in the small ballroom. The floor was swept and chairs taken down and stored. Much easier to take things down than to set them up. They kept the garlands and archway used for decoration in place. It would remind the students and staff of the Showcase experience this next week when the Kellys remained for coaching sessions. They would work with the staff during the normal meetings and dance sessions – then on to help the students signed up for coaching during the afternoons and evenings.

Molly gathered up her costumes and bag after changing back into comfortable clothes. It had been a long day, and she was tired. Her long black skirt was once again topped by her oversized sweatshirt. She and Kiki walked out to the dark parking lot together. The other shops and stores in the mall were closed hours ago so the parking lot would be almost empty. Dark and empty. There sitting on the front bumper of his car was Tommy. He waved to Molly as they walked out the mall door. He quickly ambled up to grab some of her bags. Kiki frowned. "So where's Clive?" she asked sharply.

"He hooked up with Donnette Hubble," he mumbled. Molly elbowed him and his mouth clamped shut before he said anything else. He turned to Molly and announced with a grin. "I told you I'd be back. Didn't you believe me?"

Molly Ross smiled. Kiki spotted her own car and stomped off with her bag full of costumes. "Ready?" Molly asked as she stashed her bags in the back of Tommy's ten year old black Grand Am. They squealed out of the parking lot.

The Kellys were in the studio early the next morning. Joan had picked them up from Edward's condo and whisked them out to the studio in time to work with the staff for dance session. Edward and Elizabeth were not in attendance. It was no surprise to Joan but she found herself silently seething. Just forget about him, she told herself. Enjoy the training and have a good day. That would be her goal today.

Glen began the dance session with a Tango amalgamation. It challenged and delighted the staff who found themselves laughing and intrigued by the techniques and interesting patterns. Clive was partnering with Kiki who in spite of her attempts to give him the silent treatment found herself so fascinated by the movements she couldn't stay hostile for long.

"This is a fine sequence," Clive nodded as he attempted to put together the patterns.

"And if you hadn't gone off to the clubs the other night, you would have enjoyed an even better show!" Kiki hissed. "This is nothing!" She rolled her eyes.

Clive ignored the remark and tried the amalgamation again. This time Elena came over to correct a few of his lead positions. "Try it like this," she suggested moving into dance hold with Clive and adjusting his arms and topline. "That's better," she said. "Now try it again." She frowned and again adjusted his position. "Again," she ordered.

Anna Smith danced the amalgamation smoothly with Ashley. Glen asked the pair to demonstrate, and the staff from both studios nodded approval as Anna twirled and tilted expertly into the Tango moves. She had such complete balance and grace as she glided around the floor. Ashley was in heaven to partner with such a superb dancer, and his smile was electric.

Joan and Megan stood together smiling at the performance. They both had known Anna for many years and knew what a talent she was. It was always enjoyable to see reactions to an Anna Smith performance from novice teachers who didn't know of her reputation. Glen and Elena smiled as well. They had watched

Anna compete many times in the past. Ashley was positively breathless after dancing with Miss Smith. She humbly accepted the compliments of the staff as they clapped their approval.

When the students began to arrive for their coaching lessons with the Kellys, the staff was totally enthusiastic for the lessons to begin. Those who were not teaching were invited to observe the lessons the Kellys were coaching. Glen was working with one of Anna Smith's students, and Elena was teaching Molly's country western student in the back ballroom.

Clive Forbes was in the front ballroom with Donnette Hubble. Donnette was energetic and giggling as the two warmed up with a Swing. Her blond curls bounced as she performed the quick dance with athletic precision. Her tight muscular legs naturally kicked into a relaxed back step as Clive turned her to the right and then to the left. Although a young nineteen or twenty years old, she dressed more like a junior high cheerleader with a short pleated skirt and a fluffy cropped mohair sweater.

Glen Kelly wandered into the small ballroom and stopped to watch the pair. He nodded his approval and then introduced himself. "I don't believe I saw you dance the other evening," Glen addressed Donnette.

She blushed. "I'm only a beginner," she confessed. Clive nodded but added, "She is quite talented though." Glen nodded again.

Donnette and Clive changed the music and began to dance a Cha Cha. Edward Garrett and Elizabeth scurried in, Edward to his office and Elizabeth to hers. Elizabeth stood in her doorway watching the lesson. Glen was complimenting Donnette on her

Cha Cha as Kiki Mays stood in the teachers' office doorway. The lovely Donnette was surrounded – Elizabeth in one doorway and Kiki in another. Neither looked particularly pleased at the attention the young blond was receiving from both Glen and Clive. The two were discussing in excited detail the ability Donnette possessed with her dancing. Glen called Edward over when he emerged from his office – patting his curly toupee into place and smoothing out his beautifully tailored jacket as he passed a mirror.

"I believe you should consider putting this lovely lady into a teacher training program," Glen began when Edward joined the group. "She is a wonderful dancer, and just a beginner! Imagine when she has some real training. She could be such an asset to your staff."

Edward pondered. Kiki scowled. Elizabeth frowned. Clive grinned.

"You can certainly wait for a bit, but that is my suggestion," Glen vacillated when he began to see the hesitation in Edward's response. "She is a talent you should utilize."

Donnette Hubble cleared her throat. She wasn't noticing the reaction of the others in the room. She was pondering Glen's suggestions. "I have a full time job. I was just hired. It's a great job... My parents are really encouraging me in this new career... I just dance for something to do. It's something to help me socialize and meet people now that I'm out of school." She began to ramble and wring her hands. The whole thing was putting her into a difficult situation. She was caught between her parents and these people. What would she do?

"No need to worry, my dear Miss Hubble," Edward Garrett gushed as he leaned in toward her with a smile. "We are happy to have you as one of our most prized students."

"Of course," Clive agreed. "We would like to really get some championships under our belts before thinking about turning professional, Miss Hubble. You could easily win a whole lot of gold medals in almost any category you move into."

"And then later on, if this is something you really find you enjoy, we would love to have you join the staff," Edward announced again smiling broadly. Kiki sighed. Donnette blushed girlishly. Elizabeth continued to frown.

When the lesson was over and all had walked off to attend to other matters, Elizabeth slithered across the floor like a snake to a warm rock. Clive was putting away Donnette's black dance program. His back was turned as he bent down to put the folder into place in the correct alphabetized order.

"So you prefer the girl next door cheerleader type?" Elizabeth's voice oozed her venom.

Clive was silent for a moment and then sliding the program into place pulled up to his full height. He slowly turned and responded with "I prefer any type." His eyes narrowed to slits.

Elizabeth and turned to walk away but mid-floor turned her head to make sure he was watching her walk away. She was wearing three inch high stiletto heels and a short tight skirt that hugged her behind. She smiled – he was still staring after her. Good.

Clive headed to the teachers' office. Just inside the door Kiki was perched on a chair studying her schedule. Had she witnessed the exchange he just had with Elizabeth? He sauntered over to his desk space and sat down ignoring her for a few moments.

"I thought we might go dancing tonight," he announced quietly without lifting his head to watch her response.

"What did you have in mind?" There was a slight edge to her voice.

"I know a quaint Latin club in St. Paul that has a small dance floor but very few people. We could have the whole floor to ourselves." He was fishing. Could he make it enticing enough to go some place where no one else would see them together?

"Sounds great," Kiki said flatly. She continued to write in her program.

Had she seen the conversation with Elizabeth or not? She had accepted the invitation but not given away anything in her voice or reaction. He would have to wait until the evening was over to pry any further. "Good, it's a date then?" he knew the "date" word would seal the deal.

"My car I suppose?" Kiki knew in spite of his mature appearance, Clive didn't drive nor did he own a car. He depended entirely on his friends for rides. She had always accepted the fact that he was a leech. It was just a little bit more annoying tonight than most evenings.

"I'm all yours," he slid in one of his well used phrases he thought gave him charm.

No response from Kiki Mays.

IX.

Megan and Anna carried in boxes of supplies and student cards. This space had never looked so small before. Of course, Edward was missing. Whenever there was a situation that might include conflict – and this was certainly one of those – he was conspicuously gone. Moving into a space designed for one studio and staff was definitely a situation bound to bring some frustration. They plunked their boxes onto the top of the reception desk and went back to the parking lot for another load.

Joan Ericson was there to help with the move as was expected but her staff was missing. She spotted the pair at the front desk and ambled out of her office to join in the attempt to arrange the move in. The whole idea of having both studios here had originally been frustrating, but now with the decision made, she was determined to make the best of it. Having Anna and Megan here was certainly going to be helpful especially with Elizabeth Tomlinson as her "right hand man". Elizabeth had already proven her worth to be – well, worthless. A sounding board would be welcome especially after some of the events of the past week.

Elizabeth had still not bothered to come to staff dance sessions. A non-dancing executive was always trying. Were there situations when this was a reality in this business? Of course.

Joan had known of several studios who had hired people who were not dancers for their management staff, but those people had been business people – people who knew about dealing with people. Elizabeth had no redeeming qualities as far as Joan could see other than her appearance. Men, both young and old, drooled over her looks but that didn't mean she was able to enroll any of these men as students in the studio. No, they weren't interested in dancing after getting a glimpse of Elizabeth. They were now interested in dating. Elizabeth would be a perfect addition to a dating service Joan concluded. And this studio was not selling dates. It was selling dancing and elegance and social contacts and confidence. Elizabeth was clearly not aware of their product. It was very frustrating.

Joan grabbed a box and looked around for a spot to put it. They would have two receptionists now trying to squeeze behind a normally spacious area in the front waiting area but what about their supplies? She had arranged for a few long tables to be placed in the tiny side dance studio usually used only sparingly for dance lessons. This would have to be turned into a space for some of the downtown teachers and supplies. She hoisted the box, carried it to the room and plopped it on one of the tables.

"Megan and Anna," she called to the two as they brought in more boxes. "I've set up some tables here for you to put supplies. And I've made a pot of fresh coffee for us back in the kitchenette." They toted the remainder of the boxes to the small dance studio. "I guess we can put one of the receptionists in here when it gets to recording lessons to the student cards." The two downtown executives nodded in agreement.

"This is going to be tight," Anna shook her head. "And what are we doing to do with Tournament coming up?"

Tournament was a time when the two studios joined together for special dance parties. It was a time for themes and fun – an opportunity for their students to see how to use their newly acquired dance skills in a social situation. And for the advanced students who had been around for a while, the Tournament was a time they enjoyed spending more time with friends from the other studio as well as the staff. There would be decorations and special routines.

"I was thinking about that," Joan glanced around the studio space. "It will be very claustrophobic to have everyone here and then on top of that trying to decorate for the Tournament. How about if we take the Tournament parties out to some of the local clubs? It will make it easier and no decorating!"

"Works for me," Megan chimed in. "I love the idea."

Molly Ross happened in and stood in the doorway of the small ballroom. She wore heavy winter boots, an oversized black wool coat with a striped scarf wrapped tightly around her neck, and a matching hat propped on her head.
"I forgot today's the day," she grimaced. "Should we clear some space in the teachers' office?" The teachers' office was long and narrow with heaps of dance shoes piled under each counter/desk and costumes hanging in the corner. It was generally a cluttered mess.

"Oh, hello Miss Ross," Joan greeted. "That would be nice. Oh, one more thing…".

Molly unwrapped her scarf and turned back to wait for Joan's "one more thing".

"What suggestions do you have for a local dance club that would hold both our studios for a Tournament party? Something popular and spacious." Joan peered beneath the pile of curls almost covering Molly's face.

"Well, there is Papa's." Molly pulled off her cap and unbuttoned the top of her wool coat.

"Papa's?" Joan hadn't heard of that one. She knew most clubs that had been around for a while, but she wasn't one who went out dancing socially like her young staff did after hours. "Where is it?"

"Papa's is a country western place. Very big. Lots of space for dancing, and country western dancing is the up and coming popular dance style." Molly big eyes widened. "It's out about two or three miles toward St. Paul. Not too far really."

Joan glanced at Megan and Anna who both nodded agreement. "That sounds perfect. Thanks!" Molly grinned and turned back to the task of clearing out the teachers' office.

"I think I'll call Papa's right now and see what I can arrange. Pop your stuff in this room until we can decide where everything will go," she directed toward Anna and Megan.

The move -in made the studio seem tight and crowded. The two receptionists were fighting over the phone and behind the desk space. They had to decide on a schedule leaving one behind the desk at a time to take the phone calls and schedule the

69

appointments. The other would work in the small office space recording lessons and making reminder calls to new students. It could work. It would have to work.

The downtown staff was split between the original teachers' office and the tabled work space in the small side studio. Megan and Anna would keep their work space in that side studio as well but use Joan's office when they needed to speak with a student – more professional. Elizabeth was not willing to share her office space with the two. There was a bit of bickering back and forth, but in the end Edward Garrett had sided with Elizabeth and her plea for a private office space.

"Every time she walks past us, she has a smirk on her face. She has that sickening I won haha look that makes me so angry," Megan had complained to Joan after the confrontation.

"Don't I know what you are talking about!" Joan agreed. "I have to do her job because she has no idea what to do. She is worthless."

"Why do you do her job?" demanded Megan. She shook her head and licked her bright red lips. Megan's short cropped hair with its red spikes flicked as she spoke.

"The financial issues would be horrible if I didn't. My advanced department depends on the new student department doing their job to improve our business. Without that, we're lost. So I'm going to do everything I can to ensure we have a successful studio." Joan explained although she knew Megan didn't need any.

Megan nodded her head. She understood completely. But it was knowing one person didn't pull their weight – no, refused to pull their weight by learning to do their job right. "What are we going to do when they get married?"

"Do you really think that will ever happen?" Joan's face suddenly glowed. They both knew Edward's habits and didn't expect a wedding any time soon if at all.

"Should we take bets on how long it takes for him to drop the wench?" Megan leaned on Joan's desk top and found herself grinning from ear to ear. The two of them laughed. They both needed a light moment to reduce the tension of the rest of the day.

After the first day, the studios made many compromises and adjustments but it was still tight quarters and tempers were sharp. Joan called a short joint meeting for the end of the day. Not all were excited about staying even for a few minutes longer than necessary, but they stood around the large ballroom after all of the students had exited. The receptionists sat in the corner glaring at each other. The compromises the two had made that day had been major. They were still working out their differences. Their tempers had flared frequently throughout that day.

Joan began with a cheerful "Welcome!" that was greeted with groans from most of the staff. Edward Garrett scurried in late wearing his long camel coat and interrupted the meeting.

"Excuse me, Mr. Garrett," Joan stopped him immediately. "You may speak after I am through. I have some very important announcements to make that you need to hear as well."

He tapped his foot impatiently and motioned for Elizabeth Tomlinson to stand at his side. She also wore her coat, an elegant full fur. She had hoped to skip the meeting all together. Her face pinched into an angry scowl.

Joan was not deterred by Edward and Elizabeth's moodiness. She had dealt with too much to let anything as immature as this to affect what she had to do. "First, let me commend you on your attempts to adjust to a difficult situation. I'm sure things will smooth out quickly but as they do, we will all have to work together to make this a comfortable arrangement." They all looked around at each other and forced a smile. "Let me remind you that we are in a time crunch here. The beginning of next week we have our Tournament." Everyone groaned, including Edward Garrett who had obviously forgotten this untimely event. "So to make things a bit less stressful," Joan continued," I have arranged for us to hold our first Tournament party at Papa's." The group murmured and someone actually started clapping.

Edward's face twisted as he thought this through. Joan nodded at Edward and continued. "Papa's, for those of you who don't know, is a very large country western club not too far from here. We will have plenty of space to dance and the country western theme will give us perfect opportunity for costumes. I have spoken with the management there and have arranged for us to do a staff country routine during the party. So Anna, if you could put together a Cotton Eyed Joe or maybe a Two Step for the staff to perform?" Anna nodded with a smile. Easy.

"And now, Mr. Garrett, it's your turn for comments and any other announcement…". Joan turned the meeting over to Edward.

Edward stepped forward releasing his hold on the still impatient Elizabeth who was rolling her eyes and stroking the collar of her fur. Mr. Garrett cleared his throat and smiled broadly at his staff. "I also commend you for your patience in this joining together of our studios for these very few short weeks." He emphasized the "very few short weeks" part of his speech. Then he continued. "I look forward to the Tournament party next week at Papa's. Well thought out solution," he commended nodding to Joan who smiled back. "Now for my big announcement… Elizabeth and I will be marrying in a week and a half – the Saturday after the Papa's party. So you are all invited to our celebration!"

Joan, Megan and Anna's faces showed shock but not as much as Elizabeth's. Obviously Edward had not discussed the new plan with his lovely fiancé. Elizabeth's eyes widened in surprise and her mouth gaped open. Edward turned to give her a loving glance, and she quickly regained her composure. She fluttered a hand in Edward's direction as the other hand covered her mouth. She tried to smile and bobbed her head at the stares from the staff.

Edward and Elizabeth left abruptly with the lovely fiancé hanging on Edward's arm and pulling her fur collar up around her neck. Joan could only imagine the conversation the two would have on their drive home. She had carefully studied Elizabeth's face during the announcement and had noticed the look of shock.

While the rest of the staff grabbed coats and hats, Joan and Megan huddled in the office.

"I certainly didn't expect this!" Megan paced back and forth in front of Joan's desk. "Who could have predicted this? Miss Priss is going to become our boss? Not something I want."

"And how will the wedding affect your new studio? How can he afford both? You know he won't spare any expense for the reception. That's Edward for sure," Joan was now frowning. She was imagining the two studios together for a lot longer than the month or two previously announced. The first day had been hell. "And I don't think our lovely Elizabeth had any idea Edward was planning a wedding so soon. Did you notice her face? Total shock."

Megan nodded and pursed her lips. She was now very concerned. "I could hardly stand one day with Miss Tomlinson. How am I going to stand time with the new Mrs. Garrett?"

The next few days the staff – minus Elizabeth Tomlinson, of course – stayed to work on the Cotton Eye Joe routine Anna Smith choreographed for the Papa's party. It was easy and fun to do. The partners danced around in a circle: kick, kick, triple step. Kick, kick, triple step. Triple, triple, triple, triple forward. They began in a closed dance position and then turned into a side by side position with the lady first cradled on the man's right side and then switching from right to left and back again. Then a throw out to a hand shake position. Spins down the circle line, and the couples were having fun with the country western style. Shuffle forward and practice with some boots. This routine was now melding the two studios comfortably although Megan was not any happier about the upcoming wedding, and it's affect it could have on her studio move.

X.

The winter sunset was brilliant at twilight as the staff carpooled to Papa's for the Tournament party. The parking lot was only about a third full at this early hour but would fill more as the evening progressed. It was the middle of the week, so the normal Papa patronage would be limited. With the size of the dance space, it would take hundreds to fill the club to overflowing. Joan shuffled the staff inside already dressed in cowboy attire. They looked around at the vast dance floor and nodded approvingly.

Kiki Mays wore a white cowboy hat in contrast to her creamy coffee colored skin and black hair. She chose a brilliant yellow western shirt and a denim skirt. Mr. Nelson quickly found her and invited her to dance. The huge dance floor was sparsely filled with a few dancers moving around to a two step as the music twanged. Mr. Nelson had found a red and black plaid country looking shirt to wear but was in dance shoes rather than cowboy boots.

Clive Forbes had ridden to Papa's with Tommy and Molly. Both men wore tight jeans, boots, and western shirts. Tommy's shirt was plaid with a bandana tied around his neck and Clive's was a creamy silk with brown piping and a leather vest. Molly looked overpowered in a borrowed full skirt in layers of various colors and lace hem. Her flowered blouse was billowy with long sleeves and a ruffled neckline. She had a plain bright pink scarf tied around her neck and large black cowboy boots on her tiny feet.

"Maybe you should try to dance in those boots before we have to do the routine," Tommy suggested looking concerned. After all, they were partners in this Cotton Eyed Joe amalgamation. Clive had already left the two and was trolling the room for a suitable dance partner. He slid skillfully in and out of the shadows and nooks in the room.

Anna Smith and Megan had driven over a few of their staff members. They were pleasantly surprised by the size of the dance floor. "Wow, we'll be dwarfed when we dance our routine," Anna commented as she walked around the perimeter of the floor. "That will be a change." She smiled nodding her head.

Ashley was dancing with one of his students and gave the two a thumbs up as he widened his steps when passing. He looked wonderful in a crisp striped shirt, black jeans and a western scarf with little rodeo figures around the edges. His student was equally well dressed and seemed excited by the country music playing.

Megan approached Joan who had just chatted briefly with the DJ about the routine music. "I must say, this was a great idea coming to Papa's. I don't how we could have decorated the studio and gotten everyone into that back ballroom even if it is fairly large. This floor will be fabulous for dancing." Joan nodded and then gestured to Megan to look toward the door.

Edward Garrett and Elizabeth Tomlinson had just made their grand entrance. Both were dressed entirely in white – white piped western shirts, white jeans and denim skirt, white cowboy hats and white boots. Edward wore a black and silver bolo tie around his collar and Elizabeth wore dangling pounded silver earrings that caught the spot lights in the room and splashed color everywhere. Her slim long skirt with the slit up the side gave her an even longer, leaner appearance. She looked to be an inch or two taller than Edward with her high heeled boots.

"I wonder how much those outfits set the studio back?" Megan whined as she watched them greet people and wave to those across the floor. Joan simply shook her head. "And I wonder what this wedding will cost us," Megan seethed.

The floor began to fill as students and staff arrived. They whooped at the size of the floor and clapped after each song played. The staff moved out to the middle of the floor to perform the Cotton Eyed Joe and receive the applause from their own students as well as the regular Papa's patronage. The routine ended with a whoop from the audience. Once again, the floor was crowded with dancers doing a country swing when the next song began to play.

The music was loud and the dancers laughed and hooted as another popular song began. Suddenly there was a scream. And then another scream as people began to crowd around someone who had fallen to the floor. Had someone slipped and fallen? Joan and Megan raced to the circle on the far end of the dance floor. If it was a student or staff member, it would be one disaster they didn't want to deal with tonight. They pressed through the people to see what had happened as someone else yelled "call 911". There in the middle of the group of cowboy clad dancers was Edward Garrett. He was face down with his white western hat covering his head completely. His legs sprawled and his arms limp all dressed in white like a snowman on the floor. His cowboy boots were still unworn on the soles.

"Did he fall?" Whispers were loud. "Is he OK?" Someone was bending down to feel for a pulse. One of the students was a doctor and pushed his way to the center of the crowd asking everyone to step back to give him some room. His face was grave as he looked up at the anxious crowd. "He's dead!" he pronounced.

It was now two o'clock in the morning. The body had been taken to an ambulance even though he was clearly beyond help. The police were standing around pulling yellow tape across the area where the body had fallen. The dancers were lining the walls on the far end of the dance floor giving their names and contact information to an officer before given the opportunity to leave. Joan and Megan were chatting with the detective in charge. They had already explained who they were, where the studio was located, and who Edward Garrett was. "Was it heart failure?" Joan was asking. "He's not really very old. Only forty two years old. At least that is what he tells us. He's not one to enjoy birthdays so he could have cheated a bit on the years." The remark should have brought at least a chuckle, but no one made a sound. Instead they waited for the news – the reason.

The detective looked up gravely from his notebook. "No, I'm afraid he didn't die from natural causes, ladies." The detective was formal in his tone but not heartless or cold.

"Then what happened here?" Megan could hardly contain herself. Her curiosity was peeked. "There were so many people here," she spread her arms to demonstrate. "How could it be anything but natural? Someone would have seen something. Anything!"

The detective smiled. "That's what we are hoping. We'll have to speak to all of your staff and students as soon as we can. I know it is late, so maybe we'll have to wait until morning when we'll have a clearer picture of what caused Mr. Garrett's death."

The two nodded and gathered up the staff who had ridden with them. Most were through the information line and were waiting patiently at the front door. There wasn't much to do but simply wait for a ride back to the studio. The parking lot, large as it was, was clearing out. The black and white police cars were gathered around the front door as the group moved out and into cars for the ride to the studio. Joan informed everyone they would be interviewed tomorrow about anything they noticed this evening. "It appears Edward Garrett was murdered!" she announced in a clear voice bringing a shocked gasp from those hovering close to hear what she was saying. The cool air smacked their faces as they huddled together mumbling to each other at Joan's pronouncement. Then they silently scattered to their cars for the ride back.

The next day police swarmed the studio setting up interview stations in the large ballroom. The process would be lengthy. There were close to two hundred people to interview with the staffs from both studios as well as the students who had attended the Papa's event. Everyone had to make a statement about whom and what they saw the previous evening. Joan Ericson sat in her office with the lead detective. She told him everything she could remember about the evening and had filled him in on Edward Garrett, his studio and his background. After all, who knew Edward better than Joan did. She felt pale and tried to sip her coffee calmly as he pressed her for more details.

"Miss Ericson," the detective began. "I feel I must tell you a few of the details we have discovered. But I must ask you to be discrete. Please do not confide in anyone else. We need to eliminate people before we can trust they have no involvement." Joan nodded. It would be hard, but she would have to keep secrets. At least for a while. He continued, "Edward Garrett was killed almost instantly. He was poisoned."

Joan frowned. "How could he be poisoned? Something in a drink? I don't think I noticed he had a drink. Instantly you say?"

The detective nodded. "This is the strange part. He was stuck with a poisonous dart." Again he let the information sink in.

"A dart? That is a bit bizarre isn't it?" Joan leaned back and folded her hands across her lips. "I didn't notice anything protruding from his body."

"It was very tiny. But the strange thing was the dart was tipped not with one poison but with several. The combination was what caused death to be immediate. We think the murder was somewhat knowledgeable about the effect of poisons." He waited for a response.

"Sir, we are dancers. We are not chemists or doctors or pharmacists. We are dancers. Of course, I can't say the same for our students. They are of various backgrounds. But I find it difficult to believe one of them would want Edward dead. That would be very unusual, I would think." She sighed and found herself lost in thought. Who would want Edward Garrett dead? Of course he had many vices and was irritating. But to kill him? What was the motive?

"I need you to help us." He sat back in his chair and waited for a reaction. "We need you to help us find a motive for this death. We have a suspect already."

Joan's eyes widened. A suspect? "Why? Have I been eliminated as a suspect, if I might ask?" She tried to see beyond questions and understand this last request.

"We've put together a timeline that eliminates several of the staff and students. These are people who were nowhere near the victim and couldn't possibly physically have stabbed Mr. Garrett with the dart. You were one of those we cleared, Miss Ericson."

Joan smiled. She hadn't thought about the physical proximity to Edward in order for the death to occur. "Ok. Might I ask who the suspect is?"

"You can ask," he laughed, "but I won't tell you until we make an arrest. You'll know soon enough, I think. But the question is why."

"What does his fiancé say about all of this?" she asked bluntly.

"Fiancé? What fiancé?" The detective was surprised by this last question.

"Elizabeth Tomlinson. The tall blonde in the white cowboy outfit who looks like she should be on the cover of a magazine. They were to be married this weekend." Joan was now curious.

Had no one mentioned Elizabeth? Had they not spoken to the woman?

He frowned and picked up his phone. "We saw no one by the name of Elizabeth Tomlinson and no one dressed in white cowboy attire," he finally announced after a quick phone call to someone he called "Spencer". Spencer? First name, last name, nickname? It doesn't matter.

Quickly Joan Ericson explained the story of the engagement and the upcoming wedding. She described Elizabeth and began to think again. Had she seen Elizabeth after they found the body? She didn't remember. She hadn't thought about looking for Elizabeth after kneeling near the body. The blonde woman had slipped her mind.

Just then the detective's phone rang. After a few ahs and uhhus, he hung up. "We found Elizabeth Tomlinson," he announced smugly.

"Where is she?" Joan leaned in and waited for the answer.

"Here. She just walked in as if nothing had happened." He rose and escorted Joan out to the front desk where Elizabeth Tomlinson was standing surrounded by a police escort. She looked somewhat confused staring from one person to another.

"Just what is happening here?" she twisted her head from side to side letting the blonde bang swish across her face. Now she was beginning to show irritation at the attention she seemed to be given. There was a scared twitch in her eyes as she glanced back at the police aligned behind her.

"Young lady," the detective addressed her. "We understand you are engaged to Edward Garrett."

She nodded and glared at Joan Ericson. Her eyes were asking questions Joan could not answer with the police standing right next to her.

"I'm sorry to tell you this, but your fiancé Edward Garrett has been murdered," the detective watched closely for her reaction.

"What? When? Where?" Elizabeth was not shocked, only curious with her questions. She asked if she could sit down saying she felt faint but not looking particularly weak. The officers guided her to one of the chairs in the reception area, and the entourage followed.

"He was murdered at Papa's last evening. Could you tell us where you were? I understand you arrived together." The detective put his hands into his pockets and waited for a convincing answer.

"I did go to Papa's with Edward last night, but we had a bit of a disagreement early on and quite frankly I left early with a severe headache." She looked up smugly into the detective's face and then just as quickly turned her look into puppy dog eyes, so sad and mournful. "I'm sure you have witnesses who saw me leave."

The detective pursed his lips and then let his lips widen to a grin. "I'm sure we'll find someone who saw you leave. I'm so sorry for your loss, Miss Tomlinson. By the way, just out of curiosity. Did you not notice Mr. Garrett had not returned home last night? You do live in the same residence, don't you?"

83

"Yes, we do. But I just assumed he was still angry over our disagreement. I thought I would see him here at the studio when I arrived this morning, if you must know." Elizabeth was crisp with her reply.

"And does he do this often? Not show up all night?" The detective was tilting his head to listen to her answer.

"Sometimes. Not often, of course, but sometimes," she smugly tossed her head from side to side in response. "We are like most couples and do have an occasional argument."

He nodded as if he understood completely. Then he turned motioning for his officers to release their hold on Elizabeth. They all moved back toward the back ballroom leaving Elizabeth to sit in amused silence.

The detective motioned for one of his officers. After a brief conversation, he nodded and watched as two officers walked over to Clive Forbes. "Clive Forbes, I need to you accompany us to the police station." The two officers waited for Clive to rise and standing on each side of him, walked him stiffly out to the parking lot. Clive turned his head as he moved through the door finding Kiki Mays. Her face was stony. He gave her a smile then bit his lower lip. His expression was grave. Kiki's face began to show equal concern.

So Clive Forbes was their suspect. Joan Ericson and Megan Meeker exchanged looks – curious looks. What was this about? And why would Clive Forbes want Edward Garrett dead?

XI.

"We must help Clive," Kiki Mays sat in front of Joan Ericson. "He didn't do this." Her face was determined and her voice was sharp. Considering the strained look on her face, Kiki sounded strong.

Joan sighed. She didn't love Clive Forbes like Kiki Mays did, but it was a stretch for her to believe Clive had murdered Edward Garrett. Joan nodded. "Ok, let's look at this whole thing differently. Why would the police arrest Clive? What would make him a suspect?"

Kiki sat silently for a moment. "Maybe he was near Edward just before he collapsed." They both nodded. That had to be one of the pieces to the puzzle. Other people must have identified Clive as one of the people next to Edward. "I'm going to ask questions and find out what others saw." Kiki's voice was determined.

"Just be careful who you ask," Joan cautioned lifting an eyebrow. "You might just find the real murderer in the process or find an answer you didn't want to hear." Joan didn't tell Kiki how Edward was murdered. She didn't know just at this moment if she could trust Kiki with the information. She wanted to, but Kiki was way too sure Clive was innocent. She couldn't be trusted not to blurt out the information with her questions. Joan certainly hoped Kiki knew enough to be discrete.

Kiki left the office, and Megan and Anna scurried in. They shut the door behind them and sat down. Megan's full red lips turned up into a cheerful smile. She smoothed her silky purple skirt into place as she crossed her legs. "So now the wedding won't take place," Megan began as Joan stared waiting to find the reason for this visit other than curiosity. Megan continued, "But we don't know if Edward already put Elizabeth in his will as the beneficiary of our studios." Both Megan and Anna bobbed their heads in unison.

Joan opened and closed her mouth. Hmmm. Another snag she hadn't thought about, but clearly Megan and Anna had. Now that wouldn't be very good. Elizabeth as their boss – their only boss. "Let's find out," Joan mumbled almost to herself.

The three of them stood and made their way to Elizabeth's office. Elizabeth sat inside alone with the door closed but they could see her head down on her desk through the side windows along the door frame. Joan knocked once. No answer. She knocked twice and there was a groaning sound from within. They opened the door and entered. Elizabeth's head was still resting in her hands on top of her desk. Her bang swung down over her face so all that was visible were streaks of blonde hair.

"Elizabeth, we are so sorry," Joan began trying to sound sympathetic.

Angrily raising her head, Elizabeth narrowed her eyes and demanded, "What is it you want?"

Megan was about to speak when Joan grabbed her arm and slowly shook her head then turned her attentions back to the angry woman seated in front of them. "Maybe we don't sound very sincere in our concerns," she stated in a matter-of – fact manner. "But our boss who we have known for a very many years was just

86

murdered. And the police have arrested one of our staff. So we are really in no mood to tip toe around with formalities. We are here to find out just what happened. We have noticed something very strange. You don't seem very saddened by the death of your fiancé." The three waited for her response. They all stood stiffly with clenched teeth wondering if Joan might have said the wrong thing.

Elizabeth sighed deeply. She swung her bang back away from her face. Her expression was not one of sorrow, instead it was of contempt. "I really had no idea Edward was dead. I am just trying to process this information. You are right, I did not know Edward as well as you three did," she waved her hand from one to the other. Her voice was brittle and angry. "Shall I tell you what I do know?" The three nodded briskly. "OK. I was surprised by Edward's announcement about our wedding. I really was not ready for such a quick ceremony. There was way too much to plan for. Too many things to do. The dress, the church, the reception, the cake... Not that any of you would know anything about that." Her voice was sharp and degrading. "I had no idea he wanted everything to happen so quickly. We fought. But Edward said he had it all planned. That was a surprise. He wasn't one to actually do things himself. He always had someone else do it for him. So I don't know why he was in such a rush." Again she sat back and frowned. She pounded the desk slightly. "We were having a little tiff, so to speak, last night when we got to Papa's. We wandered around the dance floor for a while so Edward could greet everyone," again a sneer when she said the word "greet". "I became bored and decided to leave. So I took the keys to the car and left. Simple as that."

"Did anyone see you go?" Joan leaned over to peer into her face.

"I don't know very many people yet," she excused herself with a sharp tongue.

"But lots of people know you," Joan added in a sugary voice.

"Touché, you have me there," Elizabeth nodded. "Maybe you should ask them and not me." Her eyebrows were raised in a way that asked the three to end this conversation and leave.

"Oh, we will," Joan smiled. "But we thought we would give you the opportunity to explain first. We wanted your side of the story. And now we have it. What will your plans be now that you won't be marrying Edward?" Ah, right to the crux of the matter.

"Hmmm. You want to know if I will continue to be your Counselor. I haven't had the time to think about it. But I will let you know when I make a decision. Fair enough?" Elizabeth rose from her chair and motioned for them to leave her office with a smirk and a wave of her diamond clad hand. It glinted in the light as she motioned reminding the three of her current position in the studio at the present time.

The three stood outside the office after their dismissal. "We still didn't find out if she inherits the studios," Megan pouted.

"No, but we did find out Elizabeth Tomlinson was not very excited about marrying Edward Garrett. Especially this next Saturday." Joan pondered this revelation. What did it mean? She would have thought Elizabeth would want the wedding to happen as soon as possible if she were only interested in Edward Garrett's money – what little there was. But did Elizabeth Tomlinson fully comprehend the extent of Edward's finances? Did she know he was broke and all his "fortune" was in his studios?

Kiki Mays made it her business to find out who had done what. Who was standing next to Edward when he collapsed. Who had initially given him attention before the doctor found him? She had to. Otherwise Clive Forbes would be the one and only suspect in Edward's death. She took careful notes after speaking with each and every person. She knew Edward fell over while speaking with Mr. and Mrs. Bell. The Bells were an elderly couple taught by one of the downtown teachers. They had been with the studio for several years now. Mr. Bell was a retired lawyer, and Mrs. Bell had been a stay-at-home wife and mother. Nothing unusual there. Clive had been standing behind the three with Donnette Hubble and Mr. Nelson. No wonder the police had zeroed in on Clive. He was standing near Edward. There was another group of students standing on the other side of the Bells and Edward. One of those students had tried to find Edward's pulse. It was a downtown student that Kiki didn't know very well. She would have to ask someone about her.

After a morning and early afternoon of studio chaos, things would have to get back to a normal schedule – and soon. Otherwise the studio wouldn't take in enough money to make payroll and pay bills. Joan and Megan would have to delve further into studio finances now that Edward was gone. Not to say the two weren't on top of things, but the final overseer of the studio checkbook was Edward Garrett. They knew what each studio took in, how many lessons were taught, and who was paid what, but the final bottom line when it came to the studio money had always been Edward. So Joan and Megan sat down with the check book and began to add and subtract numbers, call the bank and look through their own paperwork.

"Do you know how much that diamond set us back?" Megan whistled as she checked the statements. "Almost twelve thousand dollars!"

"That's a mighty big stone," Joan nodded with a grimace. "We'll never see that money again, I'm afraid. No matter what Elizabeth decides about the studio, she will never give us that pricy ring back. And I'm dreading the bill on that fur coat. And her clothes. . . . " Joan shook her head. Elizabeth Tomlinson had been a huge expense for the studios already in the short time since she first made her appearance. "Maybe her plan was to take Edward for everything she could and leave before the wedding." She laughed. Megan stared at her. "I'm only joking," Joan shook her head.

"I don't think that's a very funny joke because it sounds so plausible," Megan said going over several more of the expenses listed in the bank statement. "Oh, man. Here's another good one." She went down the list of jewels and expensive dinners on the account. "This is one serious affair for both Edward and the studios."

"It sounds like you think our lovely Miss Lizzy is our murderer," Joan looked over her reading glasses at Megan.

"I wish," Megan looked back at her and laughed. "That doesn't mean she did it, but I would love it to be true."

"Wouldn't we all," Joan agreed.

The phone rang on Joan's desk. The receptionist at the front desk was signaling her to pick it up. Joan sighed and lifted the receiver. "This is Miss Ericson. How may I help you?"

She listened for several minutes and then simply said, "I understand. Thank you."

"What was that all about?" Megan looked over with a curious frown.

"That police detective. He said they are releasing Clive Forbes. They still think he's guilty, but there isn't enough evidence at this point to hold him. He'll be back at work this evening for his regular lesson schedule. I better let the front desk know so they don't try to reschedule those appointments." She got up and headed to the reception desk to deliver the news. Hmmm. The police must have had more to go on than Clive standing near Edward before his collapse. What was it that tied the murder to Clive? She must dig further.

Joan leaned over the front desk. "Good news. Clive will be back for his lessons this evening." The receptionist greeted the news with a delighted grin and a quick sigh of relief. "Oh, and could you give me the applications we have for our current staff members. I need their whole files, please," Joan added as she draped her arm across the desk. She grabbed the stack of papers the receptionist gave her and headed back to her office. What was she looking for? She didn't quite know.

While Megan Meeker continued to complain about Edward Garrett's spending habits, Joan began to pour over the staff files.

She began with Clive Forbes. He was young. Younger than she expected even though it was she who had originally interviewed and hired Clive. She shook her head. Clive was very young indeed. Only twenty two years old. Wow. She scrolled down the other information – lives near the studio with his divorced mother and younger sister. Mother is Columbian and father is Israeli. So that's where Clive got his dark foreign look. Hmmm. Catholic Jewish mix. No wonder the marriage failed. Let's see, the father is a chemistry professor at the University here in town. Joan pondered. Chemistry professor. That must be the connection. The police must think Clive had some knowledge of chemicals, poisons and the like. That must be why they zeroed in on him. But would Clive know something because his father did? She doubted he would. After all he was just a dancer. A very good dancer, but in no way a chemist.

She knew there would be no file on Elizabeth Tomlinson, but she was a person Joan had a personal interest in even if it was just to find out her fascination with Edward Garrett. Where had she come from? And better yet, where was she going? She could ask the detective to get her some of the information she needed. Joan grabbed her phone and studying the business card of the police detective, carefully dialed his number. "Yes, I would like to schedule a meeting with you. It's important. Whenever is convenient for you. Tomorrow for coffee? Perfect! I'll see you then." Joan hung up the phone with a smile. She must gather her questions tonight.

Joan woke up with a stinging hunger in her stomach. It was one full day since Edward's death, and she hadn't eaten much the day before. She was to meet the detective for coffee at nine o'clock at a restaurant around the block from the studio. Although she normally woke late because of the studio afternoon and evening schedule, this morning was different. She awoke at seven, hurried to get in the shower and dress. Her plan was to get to the restaurant a half hour earlier than her appointment and order a huge breakfast. Her mouth watered for bacon, eggs, and a big fluffy sweet roll with gooey icing. Ah, orange juice and coffee with cream. Heaven.

Dressed in a simple black dress – appropriate, she thought for a meeting regarding a death – Joan bundled in a warm winter coat and boots. She parked in a half empty parking lot and entered the restaurant. She indicated she needed a table for two and was seated with a large menu unfolded in front of her. Coffee with cream? Thank you. That would be nice.

The table was near the door so the detective would be sure to notice her right away. She nibbled on her roll and forked mouthfuls of scrambled eggs into her eager mouth. The taste was so scrumptious. She hadn't noticed until this morning how hungry she was. She hadn't noticed how terribly hard this whole situation with Edward was. Or had been. Or was going to be.

The detective walked in and stomped off the snow from his feet as he looked around for Joan Ericson. There she was right in the front. She was finishing up breakfast and waved when he caught her eye. He ordered coffee from the waitress he passed on the way to the table.

"And how is the studio doing today?" he began as she sat down. He was a handsome man in his thirties with a muscular build and slight stubble on his chin. Efficient, to the point, and

Joan judged to be very honest. She hoped he was very honest. She was hoping he would be forthright enough to give her some of the answers she needed.

"This has been a very stressful situation. But I do have some questions I need answered. Honestly," she took a sip of coffee and watched his eyes glint.

"I also need some answers," he retorted back. "I need to know about Edward Garrett, and I think you may be the one to answer those questions." Both leaned in a bit to avoid any stray ears from eavesdropping in on a very private conversation.

Joan sighed. "I have worked with Edward a very long time. We don't always see eye to eye on things, but we did have respect for each other. That was the glue that kept our working relationship together. Believe me it wasn't easy. He could be difficult." Joan was blunt. "Ask away. I'm ready to answer your questions if you can find answers to mine." Joan braced herself.

"Who would benefit from Edward's death?" The detective was direct and to the point. He gazed at her face hoping for a glint of expression to this first question.

"That is a good question. It would depend on who inherits the studios of course. He has a new fiancé. Someone young he hasn't known for very long. If she inherits the studios, it wouldn't be until after the wedding I suppose. So I guess she would want him alive until then. Maybe he willed her his business before the wedding. That's what I need to know. What does Elizabeth Tomlinson get from his death if anything?" She had asked one of her questions in answering his. "Beyond Elizabeth, I know people had problems with Edward on a situation by situation basis, but

94

nothing that dragged on. We've all had our struggles with him. Edward could be difficult. He made decisions sometimes that didn't benefit anyone but himself. He could be very self-centered at times. Then at other times he was very complimentary and generous. Unfortunately those times were not as often as they could have been. But Edward had a sense when we needed that special compliment. He knew when we were down at the bottom and needed a hand up. That was his gift. Of course, on the other hand he spent too much money, always put the studio management into a tizzy to try to get things back on track, and sometimes had a very bad temper. But he was a character who was unique. He was someone who just kind of jumped off the page if you know what I mean." Joan smiled as she thought about Edward and his crazy personality. She bowed her head and even let out a slight chuckle.

"So just about everyone could be a suspect?" The detective looked somberly at Joan. Joan laughed and nodded. "Great! That gives me a long list again."

"So why is Clive Forbes at the top of that list, and if you think he did it, why start a list again?" Joan asked. "You have no evidence? Is that the problem?"

"Partly. He was there, I guess. But so were lots of other people."

"And his father is a chemist so he would have knowledge of the poisons?" Joan ticked this thought off without thinking she should not be quite so forthright.

"So you figured out that part of it, did you? Not really very strong evidence, do you think?" he leaned in so their conversation would be more private.

"No. And frankly I don't think Clive really has all that much knowledge. He's a dancer."

The detective shrugged. "Ok. Give me a new list."

"Well, I can't stand the fact that he's put his new fiancé onto my management team with absolutely no experience and without consulting me first. It cuts into my personal income and hinders the running of my studio." Joan lifted one finger to indicate each person on the list. "Megan Meeker and Anna Smith, the downtown studio management team, are currently in our studio struggling away until they move into their new space with a tiny dance floor, and they don't even know if Edward has – had – the money to make that move. That's a bad situation there." She lifted two fingers. "Elizabeth Tomlinson. Well, I don't know what her story is but I'm here to find out. And along the way Edward has had many lovers who I'm sure have left on very poor terms. Would one of them hold a grudge? Could be. I don't know all I should about his private life, I'm afraid." Joan was breathless by this time. "Now you tell me about Elizabeth Tomlinson."

"What would you like to know?" he pulled out his notebook and began to page through.

"Where did she come from? What did she do before she met Edward? And why does she want to hook up with an older man like Edward when she doesn't seem to want to learn anything about this business even though she's now in management. Something is odd about that." She had practically memorized the questions and now they spewed out like a faucet.

"You know. I don't have answers to those particular questions. But you've peaked my curiosity so I'm going to get those answers for you. I'm going to find out." He slapped his notebook closed and rose to leave. "I'll talk to you later, Miss Ericson. Call me if notice anything I should know about, and keep your eye on Clive Forbes for me."

"Of course," Joan smiled and nodded pleasantly. She wiped away any traces of egg and icing from her mouth with the paper napkin, then drained her coffee cup.

Arriving at the studio early, Joan thought she might have the place to herself. Peace and quiet. But as she entered, the music was already playing in the smaller ballroom. Kiki Mays and Clive Forbes were dancing a lively Samba. The Brazilian dance was light and bouncy with a pulsing Latin beat. Clive led Kiki into a series of compasos across the floor in a side-by-side position, turned her back into a closed dance position and into a series of body rolls. It was addictive to watch and actually put Joan into a cheerful mood. She stood watching for a moment until they noticed her presence. They finished the dance and then Clive slowly paced the floor before gliding toward the sound system to change the music.

"Music and dancing make me forget my problems," he explained as he passed Joan. His expression looked like a scowl but it was only because his black eyebrows were so close together above the bridge of his beak-like nose. He had classic chiseled features with neatly cut in cheekbones.

"And I guess you are one who has problems right now," Joan ventured with a raise of her own eyebrows.

"I would think everyone has problems right now. This situation can't be very good for anyone," Kiki added glancing

97

between Joan's eyes and Clive's back as he faced the sound system.

"So tell me Clive," Joan stuck her neck out again. "Why would the police zero in on you as a suspect?"

Clive lifted his head apparently shocked by the question. His forehead was furrowed as he turned his head to stare at Joan with a startled but blank expression.

"Didn't think I'd ask, did you?" She grinned back at him.

"No, I didn't. But I suppose it's a good question." He shrugged as if he didn't really know but ventured forth a quick response. "I was close by I guess."

"And who else was close by?" Joan continued.

He scratched his head and frowned. "I guess I never really thought about who else was there. I was talking to Donnette Hubble and what's his name? That student of Anna Smith's from the downtown studio. Oh, I think Mr. Nelson was also standing around us." He seemed to ponder a moment. "The Bells were there, and I suppose Elizabeth Tomlinson. Can't remember who else was around." He shrugged pretending to think more when he really wasn't trying to remember anything at all.

"You actually saw Elizabeth?" Joan was now the one to frown.

"I just assumed she would be there with Mr. Garrett," again he shrugged. "I didn't really notice at the time."

"She claims to have left before he collapsed," Joan lifted a brow and waited for a response.

Clive scratched his upper lip. "You know, I don't really remember. All I remember is Edward Garrett laying on the dance floor and people bending over him."

Joan looked as if an idea had suddenly occurred to her. She thanked Clive and scampered off to her office leaving the two to continue with their dancing. Kiki Mays seemed pleased to have Clive back in the studio. She was so attentive and …what was the word? Oh yes, fluffy. That's what Kiki was "fluffy". No longer concerned with learning the truth, she simply believed Clive was innocent and there would be no more worries. She had done her job.

Joan made a few phone calls. The last one was to Edward Garrett's condo. "Elizabeth?" she began when her call was answered. "I know this is a trying time for you, but we are going through plans for Edward's funeral. I'm sure you want to be a part of this. When can you be in?"

Joan paced back and forth from her office to the reception desk waiting for Elizabeth Tomlinson to arrive. Her biggest fear was Elizabeth had nothing to keep her around now that Edward was gone. No matter what her original plans had been in hooking up with Edward, Joan knew it was up to her to keep the woman in the studio – just in case Elizabeth was involved. Joan actually hoped Elizabeth had murdered Edward. It was no shock Joan never had a good feeling about Edward's relationship with Miss Lizzy. But if Joan thought she needed some more time to snoop any further into the murder, Elizabeth needed to remain in town and in the studio. It was that simple.

Elizabeth stalked into the reception area an hour after Joan's call. She was not in a very good mood. Her fur coat was flung over a less than perfect outfit. The knit shirt she had paired with a pair of black pants was wrinkled and plain. She wore a pair of short boots with low heels and her normally perfect swinging hair style looked stringy. She glared at Joan from ringed dark circles under her eyes and hadn't bothered to put on lipstick giving her face a pale blotchy appearance.

"So glad you could make it," Joan greeted her way too cheerfully. "The police detective will be here shortly to talk with us about Edward's funeral arrangements."

Elizabeth sighed and stomped into her office to fling her fur across a chair. She tried to fix her face with a touch of make-up and slid her fingers through her hair to plump it a bit. By the time the detective hurried through the front door, Elizabeth Tomlinson had transformed herself to a fairly presentable grieving fiancé. She even managed to plaster a smile across her face when he greeted her and give him those sad eyes of sorrow. It was quite convincing.

Joan ushered both of them into her office and purposely sat in her chair – the chair of a person in charge. Elizabeth slid into one of the chairs facing the desk, and the detective unbuttoned his coat and said he preferred to stand. He began by addressing both women. "We will have to do a complete autopsy on Mr. Garrett's body of course, with the manner of death and all." Both women nodded knowingly. "That will probably take up to two weeks. So we won't be able to release the body until that is completed."

100

Joan pulled out a sheet of paper and began to take notes. Elizabeth glanced at Joan's attention to detail and tried to look more somber, wringing her hands and twisting the diamond ring that remained on her finger. She reached for a tissue from the box on Joan's desk and dabbed her eyes letting the mascara pool a bit on her cheeks.

The detective continued with his report. "We've contacted Edward's parents...". Elizabeth's face showed sudden shock, and she cocked her head to the side to listen more attentively. "They are both rather elderly, and it is difficult for them to travel. So they will remain at home until the funeral. And by the way," he leaned in toward Elizabeth, "they are very excited to meet you, my dear. So you both will have to keep in contact with them informing them of any and all details." Joan nodded and made more scribbles on her paper. "Edward's son will also be attending the funeral." Elizabeth's eyes once again widened in surprise. "He lives in California attending college, so he will also wait until the arrangements have been made to travel so his trip won't be so extended. He needs to be back in school as soon as possible but wants to be able to go through everything in the condo with you, Elizabeth. He also invites you to live there until everything has been cleaned out and divided." He paused for a moment and then turning toward Elizabeth with a frown. "I take it from your reaction that you didn't know Edward had a son." He waited for a response.

"Oh, of course, I knew," Elizabeth recovered quickly not wanting to appear uninformed about her future husband's life. "I just had forgotten all about him. Of course he will come for the funeral. Of course!" Her voice began to rise and become breathy. Joan again wrote more notes on her paper.

"So let me repeat this," Joan said studying her paper. "We will wait maybe up to two weeks for Edward's autopsy to be completed before planning his funeral. We will keep in contact with both Edward's parents and his son about the arrangements. In the mean time, Elizabeth will remain in Edward's condo until she and the relatives can divide his belongings."

The detective nodded. "That is a good summary. And of course, we will need to keep in close contact with everyone involved in this case. Miss Tomlinson, I assume I can contact you here each day at the studio if I have any further questions?" He leaned in again to catch her answer which was a soft "of course". Her bangs flopped over her face, and she tried desperately to fling it back away from her cheeks. Her formerly huge smile was now a thin line pressed tightly into a fake grin. "And now I need to prepare for my day," she announced and excused herself abruptly.

When she was gone the detective turned to Joan and with a smirk and whispered, "I hope that is sufficient to keep her here and under your watchful eye." Joan smiled and nodded.

"By the way," Joan asked as they walked to the front door. "Did you find any witnesses who might have seen Elizabeth leave Papa's early?"

"Yes, there were several. The Bells said she left a few moments before they began their conversation with Edward. We are checking on how long it would have taken for the poison to work in his system before his collapse. Then we'll be able to see if there is any chance she might have administered the dose that killed him before she left. But so far it appears she is in the clear, I'm afraid." He shook his head. "So far, Clive Forbes is our only suspect. So keep your eyes and ears open."

Elizabeth Tomlinson was of no use to the studio that day. She hibernated in her office and saw no one except the receptionist when she ordered her to bring her coffee and donuts from the restaurant at the end of the mall. Joan had to pull out a few dollars from her own purse to reimburse the receptionist who had forked out her own money for the snack and was not pleased at the added expense.

Tommy and Molly waited until the end of the evening before knocking on Joan's door for a private chat. The two of them rocked back and forth from foot to foot debating what to say next. "What can I do for you?" Joan looked up peering over her reading glasses at the pair.

"I don't know if this is important," Tommy began looking over at Molly for support. "But we saw something last night that might be important."

Joan took off her glasses and waited. What had they noticed?

"We went dancing again at Papa's last night. The place was crowded – really crowded because it was closer to the weekend. They have a Thursday drink special, too. And it seemed very dark with all the extra people. But we saw someone. At least we think we saw someone," again he looked at Molly.

"Who did you see?" Joan frowned.

"We think we saw Elizabeth Tomlinson," Molly continued. "She didn't really look like herself, though. She wore dirty old worn out jeans and old hiking boots with a sweatshirt."

"No, that doesn't sound like the Elizabeth I know," Joan shook her head.

"She didn't have on any make-up and wore a cap that kind of hid her hair. But we really thought it was her," the two of them nodded in agreement.

"Then what happened?" Joan leaned in with furrowed brow.

"She sort of snuck in and moved around the back of the room along the wall. We tried to dance around the floor to get a better look, but she was really sticking to the shadows."

"Can you do me a favor?" Joan asked. The two of them nodded. "Keep an eye out for that woman and let me know if you see her again. It may or may not be our Lizzy, but I'd like to know for sure. You know my number both here and at my house. And thanks." Joan smiled and stood to commend their efforts.

Joan peered out her door as they left. Kiki Mays was clinging to Clive Forbes arm as they joined Tommy and Molly on the way out to the parking lot. Joan wandered out the door to observe them heading to their cars. Molly jumped into Tommy's big black car. Joan shook her head. She didn't know what was happening there with those two, but she never liked to see someone's marriage in jeopardy. Molly was so young and so newly married. She hoped this relationship was nothing more than friendship, but the other type of relationship happened so often in this business. Then her eyes searched through the darkness for Kiki and Clive. Kiki's car was right in the center of the parking lot. Clive seemed a little hesitant to get into the car on the passenger's side. Kiki was gesturing with her hands and seemed to be pleading with him. His face was – what was it? Bored? Yes, that was it. Clive seemed bored. He tilted his head to the side picking up the light above from the parking lot and seemed to be looking around the lot checking out the other cars still parked. Finally, he gave in and got into the car. He had once seemed so pleased with Kiki's belief in his innocence and so grateful for her attentions, but now she was becoming too annoying. A pain in the butt. That's what his face seemed to say. She was becoming only tolerable. Joan vowed to pay more attention to those two tomorrow. There were only a few cars still in the parking lot. Joan studied each carefully. Which car was Elizabeth driving? And was she still in the studio? Joan had been so caught up with her conversation with Tommy and Molly, she hadn't noticed if Elizabeth slipped out. It was the end of the evening so she had every right to leave. There was nothing unusual there.

Elizabeth's office door was closed and the door was shut. Joan walked over to the door for a quick check. She tried the doorknob. It wouldn't turn. Locked? Who locked their door? Joan didn't even know they had keys for these doors. Hmmm. What was inside that was so secret the door needed to be locked at night?

XII.

The studio was surprisingly pleasant. At least for the moment. Kiki was in early preparing for a lesson that involved special choreography. She had a habit of grabbing a teacher as they walked through the small ballroom to try a new move with her when she was choreographing. And her choreography was always superb. This morning she had grabbed Anna. Anna Smith loved trying Kiki's new ideas. Kiki had just led her into a Rumba back spot turn with a turn behind her back. Anna hooted her approval.

"Ooh, I love that. Try it again!" she begged as Kiki danced a little jig that her move worked so nicely.

"Ok, ok. Now add this to that…". Kiki did her back spot turn and turned Anna behind her back then into an opening out with a swivel out. "Do you think Mr. Nelson can do this?"

"Absolutely! That's a great amalgamation, and he is very talented. He should do well in the next competition. I predict a first place finish for that man." Anna nodded. "Do it again!"

Clive dragged in shuffling his feet, hands in his pockets, head down. He walked right by the two women dancing which brought a scowl to Kiki's face. Anna nudged her and whispered, "What's wrong with him? You'd think he'd be overjoyed to be out of jail and free to do what he wants."

"Yeah, you would wouldn't you? I don't know. He was suddenly sulky and moody last night. I tried to sort of be there for him, but he only wanted to go home and be alone." Kiki shrugged her shoulders but it wasn't just a so what thing. She was clearly concerned that Clive was not confiding in her. She sucked on her lower lip and led Anna once again in the Rumba move but it wasn't with the energy she had shown earlier. It was mechanical and stiff.

Elizabeth Tomlinson walked in with a new strut in her step. Unlike yesterday, she was dressed elegantly in a stunning blue dress belted tightly at the waist and matching blue pumps. She had her luxurious black fur slung over her arm. "Greetings ladies," she cheerfully chirped as she passed the two on the floor. They both stopped in mid step and froze. Joan stared out her door at the whole scene. She just happened to be more alert today vowing to listen carefully to other conversations. She was keeping her ears and eyes opened, and this was an amusing yet puzzling occurrence.

Miss Lizzy strutted by stopping at her office door. Joan peered out her own door. Would Elizabeth unlock the door? Would she use a key right in front of all of the people in the ballroom? Elizabeth stopped and stared at the door, smiled, and turned abruptly. She wandered through the ballroom and entered the teachers' office. This was another first! Elizabeth rarely lowered herself to mingle with the common people. Joan waited and watched.

At first there was silence. Then there were sounds of an argument. Between Elizabeth and Clive? Who else was in the teachers' office? Suddenly Ashley scurried through the door and made a ghastly face. Ashley could at times be a little too animated, but this time it seemed warranted. The noise continued from the office. The door flew opened, Elizabeth emerged still carrying her fur and announced as if nothing had happened, "Coffee anyone?" No one answered. Mouths were agape staring.

Elizabeth strutted out the door and down the hall for – evidently – a cup of coffee.

Joan saddled up to Ashley who was standing with his hand over his mouth staring at the closed door. "What just happened?" she demanded.

"I don't quite know. Elizabeth suddenly walked in and shut the door really hard. Clive had his head buried in his hands and wasn't paying attention, but she changed that in a hurry. She sort of hissed at him."

"What do you mean 'hissed'?" Joan asked.

"She came up behind him and began to ask questions close to his ear. He just covered his ears and closed his eyes like he didn't want to hear what she had to say. It was weird," Ashley shook his head.

"What kind of questions did she ask him?" Joan maneuvered around to come almost nose to nose with him.

"Oh, I don't know… what did you do? Why did you do that? Stuff like that. Who, what, where things." Ashley began to shake slightly. "I just got out of there as quickly as I could. I don't think she knew I was there. Am I invisible or something?" He seemed now quite insulted by this oversight on her part.

His hands smoothed his clothes as he looked down at himself assessing his own appearance. He stared into the mirror and pouted.

When Elizabeth came back toting a large expensive coffee drink, she juggled her coat so her hand was not visible. With all the shifting from her coat to her drink, Joan didn't have time to notice a key, but it must have been there. The door suddenly opened, and Elizabeth flew in tossing her coat onto a chair and shuffling her purse and cup to the top of her desk. Curiosity got the better of her, and Joan knew somehow she would have to search that office. But how?

Through this whole situation, Kiki Mays stood still in the middle of the floor with a sullen look on her face. Did she know what was going on, or was she as taken back by this argument as the rest of them seemed to be? One thing was sure, Kiki didn't go into the office to comfort Clive. She remained on the floor. Her soft silky ankle length skirt seemed to billow a bit as she picked at the sides with a nervous unconscious flick of her hands. Anna touched her shoulder bringing her back to reality. Kiki managed a brief smile but stared back with a deer in the headlights expression. Back to work.

Joan knew the meeting should be starting soon. With both studios in the same space, the meetings were sometimes together and other times divided depending on lessons scheduled for the day. Today, Joan and Megan circled the tables together for the meeting inviting each staff member as they entered the small ballroom to grab a folding chair. When everyone was seated and Joan was beginning her daily announcements, Elizabeth opened her door and stood conspicuously to the side of the management team. Joan glanced up. Elizabeth was carrying a tissue and was sniffling loudly as she dabbed her nose. "What now?" was all Joan could manage to think as she stopped in midsentence to gaze at the pale blond with red tear streaks rimming her eyes streaking black mascara down her cheeks.

"Could I say something quickly," Elizabeth interrupted. Then without waiting for a response from Joan she continued. Nodding toward a sullen Clive who would not look up to make eye contact with her, she began her speech. "First, let me apologize to Mr. Forbes for my outburst earlier today. I have just been so upset by Edward's death, I felt the need to get out all of my anger. I guess I focused in on Clive because he was at one time the prime suspect in Edward's murder. I am truly sorry." Suddenly she blew her nose loudly and continued with a mournful whimper. "I apologize to all of you for my moodiness and sad disposition. It will take me a while to get over this tragedy. Please, be patiently with me." Then just as suddenly she turned and with a loud sob scurried back into her lair closing the door with a slam.

The group sat silently for a moment. Absorbing. Then Joan took a breath and continued with her meeting looking briefly at Megan Meeker who made a slight roll of her eyes – but very subtly so as not to arouse the attention of the rest of the staff. When the meeting ended, Anna began the staff dance session, and Megan joined Joan in her office for a brief meeting.

"What was that about?" Megan tried not to scream but her voice was higher than usual. "I am now totally confused by that woman. She showed not a bit of sincerity in that little act. The nose blowing and the runny make-up was a nice touch though." Megan managed a slight chuckle then returned to her prior state of frustration.

Joan nodded her agreement. The phone rang, and with the receptionist at the bank Joan immediately grabbed it and pleasantly answered, "Studio. May I help you?"

Her face began to scrunch into a frown with lots of "ah hahs" and "I see's". When she replaced the phone, she turned to a curious Megan with an unusual announcement.

"That was the police detective heading up the investigation into Edward's death. I asked him to find some background information on Elizabeth Tomlinson. Guess what he told me?" Joan paused and Megan eagerly leaned forward and motioned with her hands to continue. "He couldn't find any. There is no information on Elizabeth Tomlinson!" Joan smugly announced with a purse of her lips.

"Oh, my!" Megan drew in a sharp breath. "What does this mean?"

"Well, it means I need to get into that locked office. Oh, I forgot to tell you. Elizabeth locks her office door," Joan nodded her head and raised an eyebrow. "Strange. But there must be a clue as to who Elizabeth Tomlinson really is behind that locked door. So here is my plan. You need to get me some time behind that door."

"And just how do you think I am going to be able to do that?" Megan demanded hands placed firmly on her hips. "How about if you act as the distraction, and I try to get into that office? She would never suspect my involvement, but I'm sure she would be suspicious of you. You've made your intentions very clear."

Joan frowned but listened. "I have a possible idea," Megan smiled broadly and continued with her plan. "You tell Elizabeth I need to use her office today to do a new student interview because you are using your office for another interview. Maybe you can even suggest that she sit in on your interview to get a better idea of how to actually conduct an interview. Then you take a nice long time for that interview while I do a short one and spend the rest of the time searching." Megan looked up with a questioning grin. "I think it might work."

Joan pondered. "Let's check our schedules." They grabbed the appointment sheets and poured over the listings. Nothing tonight, but tomorrow we have two scheduled for the same time." Her voice went up into a sing song tone, and she was nodding at the idea. "Tomorrow? Should we plan on it?" Megan grinned back and nodded eagerly.

"You are convinced that Elizabeth killed Edward, aren't you?" Megan tilted her head and waited. "Otherwise why would you want to do something like search her office?"

"I would like to think that Elizabeth killed Edward, because I personally find her very annoying – and not just because she took part of my job. But I'm afraid she didn't do it," Joan concluded with a sigh.

"And why do you say that?" Megan sounded very confused.

"Because she wasn't even there," Joan pronounced it simply. "She wasn't at Papa's when Edward was killed. There's not much arguing with something that solid. She even seemed genuinely surprised when we told her Edward was dead. She honestly thought we were joking. Doesn't make sense, does it?" Joan shook her head.

Megan considered the evidence. It was overwhelming. So why should Elizabeth so carefully try to conceal something in her office? What was she hiding? It may have nothing to do with Edward at all. It might be something completely unrelated to the murder.

The day seemed to improve after Elizabeth's apology although Clive continued to be moody, Kiki seemed distracted, and Joan tried to figure out a way to approach the plan for using Elizabeth's office to Elizabeth. The opportune moment came that evening as Joan sat behind the reception desk during a receptionist break. Elizabeth strolled by with a smug look on her face and flashed Joan a fake smile. "Oh, Miss Tomlinson, I'm so glad you came by...", Joan looked up over her reading glasses. Elizabeth stopped and waited patiently for the reason Joan was so glad to see her.

"We have a situation tomorrow that has not yet come up with both studios here. We have two interviews scheduled at the same time. I was wondering if Miss Meeker could use your office for her appointment? We do like to be as business-like as possible you know when we conduct our initial interviews. Of course, I would love to have you observe my interview in my office so you could get a better idea what your job entails. Could you do that? It's at seven tomorrow evening." Joan was sure her cheerful smile was very convincing.

"Well, I suppose I could. Yes, it would be good for me to get some hands on experience." Elizabeth's voice was hesitant but something convinced her she needed to agree to this. What made her so open to training opportunities when she had previously been so defiant and stubborn when it came to doing her job? She had shown no interest at all in learning anything about the studio. Now suddenly she was almost eager to take advantage of Joan's offer.

113

Joan continued on with some positive affirmations on Elizabeth's decision to observe a new student interview. She listed all the advantages of watching someone with experience doing their job, and Elizabeth nodded throughout the entire explanation. Yes, yes it sounded very good.

Later that evening, Joan informed Megan the plan was on. She briefly gave her a nod and a thumbs up without carrying on much of a conversation. Very neat and tidy that way. Tell no one else, Joan advised in a whisper. You never know who to trust. Who knows what they will find in that locked office?

Joan felt surprisingly giddy. She wore an over-sized blouse with a colorful African safari print that was both elegant and expensive. Joan was a careful shopper always selecting each piece of clothing for its uniqueness and perfect fit. She sometimes felt uncomfortable in her own skin. When she started in the studio – years ago – she was not only youthful but slim. Now she was a middle aged woman in a sea of young people who were still slender and stylish. So in spite of her matronly appearance and added poundage, she always took the time to look her best. Today she added a slim black skirt beneath the colorful orange, gold, and green blouse. Her heart shaped face looked smooth and cleanly accented with black eye liner and her usual emerald green eye shadow. She wanted to look her best for her interview. Not that it was unusual to have an interview or two each day, but today they had a "plan". There was a purpose greater than just interviewing a new student to find their dance needs. Today they might find the answer to a growing and disturbing mystery that may or may not be related to Edward Garrett's death.

Sauntering in with an unusually pleasant disposition, Elizabeth Tomlinson dressed in a conservative manner – not her usual striking outfit that brought glances and stares. Today she wore a suit – sleek in a gray tweed fabric with black pumps and a creamy silk blouse with a bow at the neckline. She looked extremely businesslike. Her blonde bang was pulled back in a gray hair clip. Severe but effective. Her make-up was subtle and clean.

"My, my. You look ready for your first interview today," Joan complimented. Elizabeth smiled back brightly but said nothing. Instead she once again carried her fur over her arm and deftly opened her office door without notice from anyone else in the room. How does she do that? Joan watched closely but saw nothing to indicate how she managed to use a key.

As the day continued Joan and Megan exchanged looks, smiles and sighs anticipating what their search would uncover. At quarter to seven, Joan peered out her door as she spotted a young man standing at the front desk taking the questionnaire and pen the receptionist handed him. Then a middle aged woman with a tight twist of gray hair piled on her head stomped her feet at the front door and looked around the reception room. She smiled and accepted the greeting from the receptionist. The woman approached the desk and listened to the same request to fill out the form before her scheduled lesson. Joan knew her student was female, so this must be her interview. She carefully assessed the woman planning her approach. What was the woman's motivation to be here in a dance studio? Each new student was a surprise – a mystery waiting to be solved. That's what Joan loved about this business. The opportunity to meet new and interesting people was enticing.

Now to find Elizabeth and briefly explain how to follow the interview, where to sit, and what to listen for. She peered through the glass along the door of Elizabeth's office and knocked lightly. "Are you ready?" she cheerfully asked.

Elizabeth stood in the doorway and gazed at the pair of new students in the reception waiting room filling out their paperwork. "You know, I think I'd like to observe Miss Meeker's interview," she fluttered her eyelashes coyly. "I can always observe you. We're a team. I'd like to see what Megan does. She won't be here for long, so this gives me an opportunity I should really take advantage of while I can," Elizabeth smiled broadly and strutted out to the reception area to let Megan know of her intentions without looking back at the startled Joan.

Joan's face looked strained. She looked on as Elizabeth chatted with Megan giving her the "new" plan. Megan's face looked stony - grim. She glanced past Elizabeth and lifted her eyebrows connecting her gaze with Joan's also stony expression. Foiled. How had she done it? She was very sly. Joan had never recognized just how clever Elizabeth Tomlinson was until this very moment. Right now, at this minute, Joan believed Elizabeth, in spite of not being physically present at Edward Garrett's murder, was somehow involved. She didn't just have a hunch about this feeling, she knew it to be true.

Megan and the tall slender young man walked to Elizabeth's office with Miss Tomlinson tagging along behind. "I'm a supervisor," Elizabeth had explaining to the man. "I'm making sure you are well taken care of here at the dance studio." He had seemed pleased to have her along. He was young and boyish. Maybe in his early twenties with sandy blonde hair cut in a longish style and a scruffy beard and mustache that weren't quite a beard and a mustache yet. He wore simple stone washed jeans and a flannel shirt in a red plaid. Joan stared after him intently memorizing his appearance. Then she turned to face her new student.

"Ah, Ms. Greshing, I'm Miss Ericson. I'll just go over your dance goals with you before you begin your lesson so we are positive you receive just what you need to become a comfortable dancer." Joan led the woman to her office. Ms. Greshing was short and a bit dumpy. Joan discovered she had been divorced for over ten years and was just now deciding to get back into the social scene. She was lonely. Joan listened politely to Ms. Greshing's woes and desire for more excitement in her life. Her head nodded but inside she felt the anger rising. She had been sandbagged. What now?

When the interview was completed, Joan ushered Ms. Greshing to the dance floor to meet Ashley, her dance teacher. Ms. Greshing smiled politely as they were introduced and actually giggled as Ashley started her walking across the floor introducing the basic movements of dance. The tall thin young man was also out on the floor with one of the downtown teachers; Elizabeth Tomlinson was standing in her doorway observing the lesson – one eye on the student and one careful eye on Megan. Foiled indeed!

Elizabeth became like a Siamese twin to Megan throughout the entire interview, lesson, and follow-up. Never in the weeks of being a part of the studio had Elizabeth Tomlinson ever paid so much attention to procedure or the teaching of a student. Tonight was either a breakthrough or a very clever plan to protect her territory – her locked office. Joan preferred to think it was the latter. But why?

The teaching day ended. Molly Ross and Tommy McLaughlin were ready to leave. Pulling on her heavy boots and snatching up her wool coat, Molly glanced up at a sullen Kiki Mays. "Want to go to Papa's tonight?" she offered stuffing her mound of black hair under a stocking cap.

"I don't think so," Kiki sighed. "I don't much feel like doing anything right now." When Kiki was down in the dumps it was way down in the dumps. She couldn't function on any level. Kiki sat at her counter, legs splayed in front of her, shoulders hunched over.

"I thought you and Clive had gotten together again," Molly tried to sound chipper without sounding too gossipy or nosy.

"So did I but I guess not," Kiki kicked off her dance shoes and laid her head down on the counter. "I don't know what's wrong with him, but he's avoiding me big time." Clive had already managed to scamper out of the studio at the crack of ten o'clock.

"Ok, then. We're going to head out. See you later," Molly slowly dragged out the door. She felt guilty leaving Kiki. The last time Kiki broke up with Clive, she called in sick for days, and the rest of the staff had to do double duty teaching her very advanced students. Molly hoped this wasn't going to become a behavior pattern. It was not pleasant trying to teach a student who was more experienced than the teacher. In fact it was downright agonizing. Molly Ross shock her head and hoped tomorrow would not be a repeat of the dreadful few days she had spent the last time Kiki called in with an "illness".

Elizabeth Tomlinson had managed to lock up her office and sneak out early. Megan was seething. "Well, no luck on finding out what Elizabeth has hidden in that office of hers. And I'm afraid she is on to us, so we'll never get another chance," she plopped herself down in one of Joan's office chairs and rolled her eyes. Megan's ruby red lips had been recently retouched and her spiky hair re-sprayed into crisp shoots splaying from the top of her head.

"So how was the interview? Tell me what she did in that office?" Joan questioned curiously but intensely.

"She was surprisingly interested in our new student. Of course he noticed her right away and kept glancing in her direction as she smiled coyly at him. It was sickening. I had a hard time even sitting behind the desk. She sat at my elbow. I was totally tailed the entire lesson. No chance to look anywhere. I'm sorry I failed," she hung her head and scowled.

"Not your fault, dear. We were sandbagged. She knew exactly what we were doing the entire time. And I never gave her credit for any brains. Obviously, she has some intelligence. Lots of intelligence, I'm afraid." Joan tapped her pen on her desk. "Want to go out for a drink or coffee?"

"Great idea!" Megan's face lit up. "Where shall we go?"

Joan's phone rang. She cursed under her breath. Not now just when she was getting ready to leave. What could be so important this late at night? "Studio!" she answered as cheerfully as she could but with a sharp edge to her tone. Suddenly her voice became breathy and excited. "What? Really? I'll be right there." She turned to Megan and with eyebrows raised and announced,

"We're going to Papa's! That was Tommy. Elizabeth Tomlinson just turned up."

The two scurried out the door locking it behind them and out to Joan's car for a quick trip to Papa's country western club. The drive was about twenty minutes during rush hour but traffic was very light this time of night so it took no time at all. Joan had to think carefully to remember just how to get to the club. The only time she had been at the place was the night Edward was killed, so she had to recall exactly which way to go. The parking lot was about half full. They picked a spot near the entrance but slightly hidden by a bush in case they needed a quick getaway. They laughed at the implication. It was so spy-like. The thought of escaping from a country western dance club sounded extremely funny.

Once inside they looked around for Molly and Tommy. The floor was crowded with dancers some dressed in Stetsons and boots. The music was loud and the beat pounding. Most people were clapping or nursing a drink at one of the many side bars. The walls and corners were shadowed and dark. Megan spotted Molly dancing across the floor in a darkened corner. Her small stature and big curly mop of hair flashed in shadows across the walls as she moved past the spot lights periodically placed along the dance floor. Joan and Megan made their way through the crowds toward the couple elbowing and squeezing through the throngs of western dressed cowboys.

"So where is she?" Joan asked tapping Tommy's shoulder. Tommy was big and muscular so Joan had to reach up to grasp his bulky topline. He turned abruptly to face her – his surfer tanned face and bleached hair looking young in the dim lights.

"We thought we'd try to stay out of the way so she didn't spot us – if she hasn't already," he said pointing toward a dark corner way on the other side of the room. Joan and Megan nodded as they squinted trying to see who or what was in that corner. It was hard to see anything. The two slid round the groups of patrons in massive cowboy hats sidled up to the bar with tall icy mugs on the counter in front of them. Almost to the corner Tommy had pointed out, Joan stopped abruptly and stared. There seated in the corner with her back to the crowd was a woman – slender, dressed in worn jeans and a sweatshirt with a gray tam pulled down over her hair.

"I don't know," Joan shook her head and glanced at Megan who was also staring at the woman. "She doesn't look much like Elizabeth." It was noisy and hard to hear, but Megan understood the implication of what Joan was saying. "Let's stay back here along the wall and wait. I want to see her face." They nodded to each other and scrunched back behind a group of people laughing and talking loudly about a football game or something. They waited for what seemed to be a long time. The woman sat without moving – without talking to anyone around her. Strange. Then after about forty-five minutes a slim tall man sauntered toward the corner and sat down right next to the woman. He wore cowboy boots, a plaid flannel shirt and a large Stetson. When he lifted the hat to smooth down his hair, Megan gasped.

"That's my new student – my interview tonight!" she hissed into Joan's ear. They looked at each other with confused expressions. Then the Elizabeth look-a-like and Megan's new student got up and headed toward the door. When the woman turned briefly to ask the man trailing her a question, Joan stared at

121

her face. Plain with no make-up, she did have the features of Elizabeth Tomlinson. Was it Elizabeth? Could she have a look-a-like or a twin? Joan grabbed Megan's arm and silently motioned for them to follow. They tried to stay back as far as they could without losing sight of the pair. The front door loomed ahead with a slight glow of light that illuminated their faces. It could be Elizabeth. Maybe? Joan squinted and stared but couldn't make a definite decision. They slid out the door and searching the parking lot finally spotted the two slip into an old rusted Oldsmobile of an indescribable color and take off with a squeal of the tires out of the lot.

"Let's look for Elizabeth's car because that definitely wasn't it!" Joan suggested as they watched them drive away. "Do you know what she drives?"

"No, I haven't noticed. I'm not really a car person, but I would assume it would be one of Edward's cars," she shrugged. "He has that old Caddie and that new sports car – the green one. I might recognize it if I saw it." They nodded and walked around the lot. It had filled up since they arrived, and it was cold and mounds of ice made walking slightly awkward. The wind was whipping at their faces. Inching around the closely parked cars proved to be a struggle. At one point, Megan grabbed Joan's elbow to keep her from falling and sliding under a large pickup truck with the jacked up wheels. About half way around the lot, Megan pointed to a car in the back corner. It was parked behind another large truck but the nose poked out slightly. Yes, they trekked over to the car and studying it carefully agreed it was Edward's sports car. The vanity plates reading "DANCE" sealed the deal. The woman had definitely been Elizabeth Tomlinson. Now the

122

question was why? Why was she dressed down and why was she with Megan's new student? Had they made an instant connection during the interview that evening and agreed to meet? Wow, she worked fast if that were the case. She didn't take too long to mourn Edward Garrett and his death.

"Let's go! I'm not waiting around for them to return," Megan demanded shivering as she tried to warm her hands and face with a breath of air into cupped palms. They hopped into Joan's car and started the motor to warm up.

XIII.

Molly and Tommy hurried into the studio early. Usually Molly shuffled in as late as she could, but today she was eager as if ready to burst. "Miss Ericson, Miss Ericson!" she knocked on Joan's door excitedly. Her boots left a trail of melted water on the wooden dance floor. They would have to clean that up before lessons began.

Joan was tired. She normally went home and to bed after a hard day in the studio, but the visit to Papa's last night kept her out late. The cold wind and standing around crowded parking lots wore her out. She came out of her office looking drawn, patting her hair into place and yawning ever so slightly.

"Sorry, it was a long night," but she smiled and waited for Molly to tell her what the excitement was all about. "Tell me. What's going on?" Her face pressed forward in eager anticipation.

"We got a job! I mean we got the studio staff a job." Molly still had on her heavy wool coat. She was unwrapping the scarf from around her neck. "The management at Papa's saw us dancing last night and remembered us from the other night. They want us to do some shows. Something country western. You know, a two step or country swing. Can we put something together by this weekend?"

Joan was never thrilled about shows. That had always been Edward Garrett's department. He took great joy in putting together routines and showing off his dancing staff at local clubs. He was a showman that was for sure. "Now that Mr. Garrett is dead we have to keep up all areas of the studio. Business continues as usual. So I think this is a great opportunity for us. How many shows do you think they would like us to do?" Joan nodded twisting her lips into a pucker and staring at Molly's anxious face.

"If the one this weekend goes well, I'm sure we will be able to perform every weekend or two," Tommy added to the conversation. He was standing behind Molly with a look of pride. They were the new teachers on the staff, and they had landed a big show. His tanned face was as enthusiastic as little Molly's.

Joan made a suggestion. "Let's get Anna Smith to put something together. How many do you think we should have in the performance?"

"Let's get the whole staff involved. Staff from both studios!" Tommy's face lit up. He shook his bleached blond hair, and the glow on his face showed a slight pink tone in his cheeks from the cold weather.

"Why don't you talk with Anna when she comes in and maybe she can arrange dance sessions around the routine choreography. Sorry, but my phone is ringing. Where is the receptionist?" she asked angrily spinning back toward her office. Joan raced inside to grab the phone. It was the police detective. Kicking her door closed for a little privacy she told him about her evening at Papa's. "I don't know how this all connects, but one of Edward's cars was parked in the lot at Papa's, and it sure seemed like the woman we saw was Elizabeth Tomlinson. But she was different – not the same appearance and not the same kind of clothes Elizabeth wears. Have you found out any information on her yet?" Joan shook her head. "No, huh? That's a mystery. The strange thing was it appeared this Elizabeth person we saw was with a man who came into the studio last night for a first lesson." There was a pause as Elizabeth listened. Then she pondered. "Hold on for a moment. I'll check on that for you."

She placed the phone on her desk and crossed the small ballroom to the front reception desk. She grabbed the schedules for the week and returned to her office. "Here it is. His name is John Jones. Doesn't sound very legit does it? I would guess that is not his real name. He didn't buy lessons so I am assuming we won't see him back in the studio. I guess he is a dead end. But here is the address and phone number he listed." She rattled off the numbers. She listened again and then thought for a moment before answering. "Well, he was fairly tall maybe about six feet or six one. He was very slender and had longish blond hair. It was scruffy looking. Not a professional looking man but one who fit in well at Papa's." Then she listened again. "A photo? Maybe. We could try."

After she hung up the phone, Joan vowed to check further on the student who Megan and Elizabeth interviewed last evening. He was somehow involved. But how? The detective asked if they could get a picture or even a drawing. She would have to ask Molly and Tommy once again to call her if he showed up at Papa's again. Now where was her camera?

Anna Smith was very happy to put together a country western routine for the staff to perform at Papa's that weekend. She asked Molly and Tommy to help her choose an appropriate song. They were more familiar with the new country songs. "This country western music is the latest trend. I really like it, but I'm not too familiar with the songs Papa's usually plays. What do you suggest?"

Molly picked a couple of her favorites, and Tommy had a few suggestions. After listening to some of the tunes, the three of them chose a nice song by a new singer currently making a name for himself on the country charts. They tried a few movements, a few basics, and maybe a step or two that really looked flashy. "Let's try a lift," Anna suggested. "Here's one everyone should be able to do." She showed Tommy how to lift Molly onto his hip then with a swinging motion throw her to his other side. Molly was so tiny and light to lift. Tommy was stocky – very muscular – so the lift was easy for him. "Do you think Ashley will be able to do this one?" Anna asked. "He's pretty short and not very strong. Maybe you could dance with him Molly? You are more his size."

When the staff came in, the Papa's project seemed to get them all excited. The past week with Edward's death, the mood had been rather depressed and strained. This routine brought the staff attitude up to almost "happy" on the mood-o-meter. They worked on the entrance – the start of the routine – and the basic patterns after choosing partners and arranging a formation. The Two Step moves in a circle called the line of dance – a counter clockwise direction similar to street traffic all traveling along together. Anna had the couples moving forward and then at the same time, everyone made a left turn circling in place until the men had their backs to the line of dance. Then the men danced the basic backwards until another series of left turns brought the couples back to their forward moving position again. It was very precise and fun to watch. They put in a few under arm turns for the ladies who continued moving in the same counter clockwise direction along with their partners. The style of the Two Step is to shuffle. Make it look easy and down into the floor. Real country and relaxed to fit the earthiness of the music.

While the staff was practicing their Two Step, Joan decided to have a conversation with the receptionist. Elizabeth arrived late, strolling in while Joan was seated at the front desk going over the schedules and messages. She wore a flattering winter white gourd skirt that hung to mid calf and a matching cashmere sweater with a striking caramel colored necklace and matching dangling earrings. Her streaked blonde hair was perfect as was her flawless make-up. This just didn't seem like the woman they saw at Papa's last evening. Elizabeth nodded a pleasant greeting and with her fur over her arm hurried back to her office. A few moments later, she stood in her doorway watching the dance session but never joining in. Her head began to nod to the beat of the catchy song and a slight smile crept across her face. She seemed to enjoy the music as well as the routine the dancers were learning.

127

Joan pointed to the "John Jones" name on the schedule from the previous night. "What can you tell me about this interview?" she asked the receptionist in a quiet whisper of a voice. In most cases the receptionist listens to all of the requests and explanations from students when they call before they make their appointment. The receptionist can be the most informed person when it comes to finding out about a student's history.

"That's an interesting story," the receptionist commented studying the name. She was quite young – a college student who only worked part time. She wasn't really interested in the dancing part of the business, but she loved to talk. Students would call in to the studio just to chat with her. She swung her long brown hair back behind her shoulders and stuck her chin out as she began to tell her story. "Mr. Jones wasn't originally scheduled for that appointment. You'll notice there are lots of lines erased in the schedule slot. The original appointment called to cancel late yesterday afternoon. Suddenly this Mr. Jones calls about five minutes later and says he really wants to come in last night at seven o'clock. That's the only time he's available. So I said 'we just happened to have a cancellation at that time. Can I put you in?' And he says 'yeah!' He seemed very happy to have the appointment. Then he doesn't even buy a dance program! I don't know what's wrong there. They seemed to have a good lesson and all. I was careful to explain just what would happen on that introductory lesson and that he would be able to select an appropriate program that would fit his dance needs when the lesson concluded. " The receptionist shook her head with a frown. "I would have pegged him for a sure buy." This young woman was very good at her job. She always seemed to prepare her new student callers before they came in for a first lesson, and Joan had no doubt she had done her job very efficiently in the case of Mr. Jones.

"You say he called in to take a cancellation?" Joan didn't expect an answer to her question although the receptionist nodded. She was just repeating the curious coincidence of the situation. This was something she needed to remember to tell the detective when she talked to him next time. Very curious. Very curious indeed!

Joan walked slowly back to her office watching the dancers move around the floor as they learned a new amalgamation for the routine. They had moved from the small ballroom to the larger room. With so many dancing, they needed more room to work. She motioned to Elizabeth who was still watching the rehearsal. "Don't you want to join in? You could learn the routine – they are just starting to work on the patterns."

Elizabeth smiled pleasantly but shook her head. "Looks too hard for me. I'm not that advanced yet."

"Maybe you should practice more. I'm sure the teachers would be happy to help you when they are not teaching a lesson." Joan cocked her head to the side waiting for a response. Best to take advantage of this new interest from Elizabeth.

"You don't seem to practice much," Elizabeth's hardness came back, and she was once again throwing out a barb.

"I've done lots of dancing in my day. Now it's time to let the others enjoy the opportunity," Joan was not thrown by the insult. Instead she just smiled and used it to her advantage. Elizabeth's face stiffened. The toss back had been effective. "In my day," Joan continued, "Edward had us doing show after show. I'll have to show you some of the old tapes. Edward taped everything. He was a recording nut. Everything recorded."

Elizabeth's face paled. These last few remarks about old dance routines seemed to strike a chord in her mind. She slunk back into her office and shut the door without so much as a response to Joan's volley.

Joan rejoined Anna along the wall of the large ballroom watching the last section of choreography rehearsed with the music. "I'm wondering if we could add a few more people to this?" Anna was suggestion.

"What! We seem to have a large enough staff already, and Elizabeth refuses to try something this complicated." Joan watched the mass of dancers circling the floor and go into the lift Tommy and Molly had practiced earlier.

"I know. I know, but we have a part that switches partners and it doesn't work with what we have right now. I was thinking maybe we could ask Kiki's student Mr. Nelson to dance with her and possibly Miss Hubble with Clive. Those two seem to be on different ends of the world right now, and their partnership is rather stressful to watch." Anna pointed with a nod of her head to Clive trying to lift Kiki who was looking rather like a sack of potatoes at the moment as he tried to fling her to his other hip. Normally a superb dancer, Kiki Mays was looking rather like a beginner as Clive tried to lead her in a violent half-hearted manner. Kiki was becoming more and more frustrated by the minute. Joan nodded. Something had to be done or the routine could be a disaster. This partnership could prove to be the undoing of something that could be very successful.

Anna walked up to the couple on the break and made the suggestions about asking their students to join in the routine. Kiki seemed delighted and ran off to phone Mr. Nelson as quickly as she could. Clive at first looked sullen, but then a spark lit in his eye, and he slowly smiled. Nodding his head, he finally agreed. He said he would call Miss Hubble as soon as the rehearsal was over. At the staff meeting, both reported an agreeable response from both students. Kiki seemed especially relieved with the news. They all agreed another rehearsal that evening after the studio closed was a must.

Joan felt in a dilemma. Tonight would be the perfect night to head out to Papa's with camera in hand to take a few photos of "John Jones". With the staff here in rehearsals, if the man was indeed an acquaintance of Elizabeth Tomlinson's, they would surely show up at the club knowing no one from the studio would be there to spot them. On the other hand, Joan hadn't had a chat with Donnette Hubble yet, and she had been one of the people standing next to Edward when he died. She needed to speak to Donnette, and soon! What would she do? Which place was most important? Maybe she would have to ask Megan Meeker to take part in some of this activity. Megan was only too eager to help. She thought maybe the trip to Papa's would be the best as she knew what John Jones looked like and could easily spot him. Joan nodded. Yes, that sounded perfect. She would stay in the studio and talk with Donnette before the rehearsal. They tried out the camera. It had been a long time since it had been used. Was everything in working order and could they change the settings to avoid a flash? A flash would certainly be a tip off to anyone Megan tried to photograph.

"The Lord didn't bless me with a technical mind. These settings are a mystery to me," Joan commented as she played with the camera buttons. After a few frustrating attempts, she handed the camera off to Megan who promptly clicked something-or-other that made the camera work properly. Soon everything was set and ready to go.

Megan slipped out of the studio before the last lessons were over so as not to have to offer an explanation to one of the staff who might wonder where she was going. She had the camera in hand and tried to look inconspicuous – wiping off her bright lipstick and pulling a winter hat over her spiky hair. She wrapped a black scarf around her neck and face before toddling off to use Joan's car for the trip to Papa's. Her boots slipped across the parking lot as she scanned the lot for the small compact.

Joan spotted Donnette, that cute little cheerleader type, when she first walked in the door. Clive Forbes was in the back ballroom teaching a lesson, so Joan walked out to the front reception area to greet her. Donnette looked so chipper and sweet tonight. Probably excited about the opportunity to dance with the staff in a routine for Papa's, Joan concluded. Joan took this moment to shuttle Donnette into her office for a chat.

"I just have to ask you something about the night Edward was killed," Joan began as Donnette took a seat. Donnette's face turned from cheery to stricken.

"Oh my, that was a horrible night!" she exclaimed in a high breathy voice. "I have never been so close to someone who's died before." She began to rub her hands together. "I try not to think about it." Her head bobbed back and forth as if she had a nervous tick.

"I know, I know." Joan soothed. "But you were so close to him when he fell over. I was wondering if you noticed anything unusual? Anything at all."

Donnette frowned as if in thought. She was trying to think back to that night. "Let's see, I was standing next to Clive, Mr. Forbes talking with Mr. Nelson." Edward Garrett insisted staff and students in the studio call each other by their last names. More professional and formal, he had said. Those who had been in the studio for a while continued with that practice no matter who they were speaking to or about. It became habit. Joan nodded encouraging more recollections.

"Mr. Garrett was talking to the Bells and one of the other downtown students. I think it was Mr. Harrison. Yes, it was Mr. Harrison." Mr. Harrison was one of Anna Smith's students. He had literally been with the studio since it began. Always old looking, Joan noticed through the years he never seemed to age because he had always seemed that way. She had once asked him how old he was and the number had surprised her. He was actually much younger than ancient. He just appeared ancient. Joan chuckled. Mr. Harrison was one who always spoke to Edward in a gruff manner, calling him on anything he felt was wrong with the studio. Everyone knew it was just his nature and complaining gave him something to do. It was his pleasure in life to complain. Edward actually enjoyed the banter between the two of them. It had become a pleasant diversion from the usual tediously sugary conversations with most students in the studio. Edward had relished the opportunities to speak with Mr. Harrison.

"Do you remember the conversation?" Joan prodded.

"Well, Mr. Harrison was complaining as usual. He hated Papa's and hated the country western music. Mr. Garrett was staunchly defending it as the up and coming trend in popular music. I believe those were his exact words. Then he fell forward. Just dropped over!" Donnette was tense as she recalled the moment. "I was trying not to listen in on their conversation, but the one we were having with Mr. Nelson was so boring. He's an accountant and as usual, he was talking numbers. Clive was being polite and nodding and smiling and laughing a bit, I think."

"Where were the three of you standing? I mean Mr. Forbes, Mr. Nelson and you when Mr. Garrett fell over?" Joan clasped her hands and tried to picture the formation of people at that moment.

"Well, I couldn't actually see Mr. Garrett fall until he actually hit the floor because Clive was between us. He's so tall and all that he blocked Mr. Garrett from view when the Bells and Mr. Harrison were talking with him. So the Bells and Mr. Harrison were facing us. Mr. Garrett fell forward almost hitting Mr. Bell. But he stepped out of the way when the body fell. Oops! Body.... I don't know if that was the right word." She grimaced.

"Did you notice Elizabeth Tomlinson?" Joan pushed her even further.

"You mean Mr. Garrett's girlfriend – I mean fiancé? No, I saw her earlier that evening. I saw her stroll in dressed in that white outfit, but didn't see her at all after the routine was finished. No, Mr. Garrett was standing there alone without her. Maybe she was someplace else like the rest room or across at the bar, but I didn't notice her." Donnette shook her head trying to recall the details. "Then one of the downtown students – Miss Chapman I think – knelt down on the floor and tried to feel for a pulse. I guess she's a nurse or something. Someone in the crowd happened to mention that about her before the doctor came and pronounced him dead already."

"Was Miss Chapman standing near-by when this happened?" Joan made a note of her name on a scrap of paper.

"No, there were some students from the downtown studio standing oh, say ten or twenty feet on the other side of Mr. Garrett. There was a lot of opened space between them. She had to rush over maybe ten, fifteen steps or so to get to the body. Oh, there I go again calling it a 'body'." She was very precise with the lengths and spaces Joan thought.

Donnette saw the confusion on Joan's face. "I am a student, Miss Ericson. I study interior design and room proportions are something I look at every day. I am quite sure about my distances in this situation." Donnette nodded with a very mature and knowing expression. She was now not the bubble headed cheerleader type when she spoke of space in a room. She was definite and clear in her calculations. The professional.

Joan thanked Miss Hubble for agreeing to learn the Two Step routine for the Papa's show and for the information about the night of the murder. Then she sent her off toward the back ballroom for the rehearsal. Meanwhile, Joan pulled out her piece of scratch paper and began to draw a diagram. She put Edward in the middle with Mr. and Mrs. Bell and Mr. Harrison across from him. Then to Edward's left was Clive speaking with Miss Hubble to his left and Mr. Nelson across from them. About ten to twenty feet away was Miss Chapman and a few downtown students. She stared at the drawing and pondered. She knew why the police had picked up Clive Forbes initially for questioning. He was the only one in proximity to the body who could have stabbed Edward with the poisonous dart. That is if it was an instantaneous death. Could he have been stabbed earlier and suddenly felt the effects during his conversation in this particular spot? That was a good question for the detective. She wrote it down carefully so if someone else spotted the note they wouldn't suspect what Joan was insinuating. She must be careful. Things were getting complicated. She wondered how Megan was doing at Papa's or if the excursion was a waste of time.

Megan drove all the way to Papa's with a string of cars honking behind her. She was a slow inexperienced driver who always struggled with highway traffic. Tonight was no exception. With her white knuckled hands gripping the steering wheel, she ignored the cars whizzing by her giving her dirty looks. One of the reasons she loved to teach in the downtown studio was the convenience of the buses. She took the bus everywhere. And now that she was out in the suburbs, the bus route each day was complicated. First one bus and then a transfer to another. It was an experience she hoped would change as soon as they moved into their new space. Speaking of the new space, she and Anna would have to follow up on the progress of the new construction. The normal fifteen to twenty minute trip to Papa's took Megan Meeker thirty-five long and painful minutes. But it would be worth it, she

136

surmised as she patted the cameral next to her seat. Finding a parking spot was relatively easy. She wanted to stay back in the shadows again if possible, and with such a cold evening, most patrons were parking as close to the door as they could. So the back spots were open and available. Megan pulled the car into one with lots of space around it in a back corner. She hated parking in a crowded lot so looked for the spot easiest to pull out of later when it was time to leave.

The camera was small and inconspicuously slid into her coat pocket for easy removal. She crunched across the icy parking lot with her Minnesota winter boots and scurried in through the front door. Standing along the front wall to allow her eyes to adjust to the darkness, Megan scanned the dance floor first. Why hadn't she first looked for that beat up old rust bucket of a car they had seen John Jones drive away in the other evening? Would she have recognized it again if she saw it? No, the parking lot seemed filled with beat up old rust buckets and pick-up trucks. They all looked alike to Megan who claimed to be no car whiz.

No one on the dance floor looked like the tall lean blonde who she had interviewed the other evening. So she carefully walked around to the other side of the dance floor scanning the walls and bar areas. Best to check the place they saw him last time she and Joan were in looking for Elizabeth. She slid around to the other wall and peered into the dark corner. There were several people seated in a grouping. She couldn't see most of them as they sat with their backs to her. Maybe she could move around to the bar and get a better look from that angle.

She sauntered up to the bar and the quick acting bartender immediately slapped a napkin down where she was standing to ask

for her order. She ordered a diet soda, and he quickly obliged.
Megan fished in her pocket for a buck or two to pay for the drink
letting her eyes momentarily stray from that corner. "By the way,"
she asked as she slid her money across the bar top. "Have you
seen a man about six feet, skinny and scruffy beard? Longish blond
hair with maybe a cowboy hat?"

The bartender laughed. He was young but big and beefy
with dark hair and a friendly bartender-like grin. "That sounds like
almost everyone in this place?" He gazed back in a friendly
manner, but then nodded over a few spaces down the bar. "But
that guy who just ordered the beer sounds a lot like the man you're
looking for."

Megan glanced to her left. Indeed down the bar was a man
who was just paying for a bottle of beer. He turned and walked
back to a darkened corner of the room. The man indeed was John
Jones. Megan quickly turned away so he wouldn't notice her. If
Elizabeth Tomlinson were with him, Megan was going to have a
difficult time getting close enough to get his picture. Sure enough
walking out of the lady's rest room to join "John" was a woman
looking very much like the studio's Miss Tomlinson. What now?

Megan twirled on her barstool letting her legs dangle freely
and faced the bartender who was wiping the counter in front of her
soda. "Listen, I know this sounds strange, but I need to get a
picture of that guy over there. The one who bought the beer, but
without him knowing anything about it. What do you suggest?
You seem like a smart guy," Megan gazed into his intense brown
eyes and watched him twirl the ends of his black mustache. He
was a big man who could easily have been the bouncer rather than
the bartender. He filled the space behind the bar with little room

for anyone else to squeeze along side of him. She pulled the camera out of her pocket and motioned for him to come closer.

"What is this?" his eyes narrowed leaning in with his bushy eyebrows touching above his nose in a curious expression. "Some kind of a cheating husband?"

"Yeah, something like that," Megan lied. "I just need his picture without him knowing it was taken." She pulled out her wallet and absentmindedly searched through the bills making sure he noticed the wad of money was substantial although it was only a pack of ones she used for her many bus trips to and from the studio.

"Wait here," he nodded, grabbed the camera and slid down to the end of the bar. He whispered something in the ear of the waitress picking up her tray of drinks. She frowned but nodded. He proceeded to follow her across the room all the while snapping pictures of her. She was a lovely woman with a slender body, pretty face, and a head of long luxurious hair curling down her back. Her short white apron was tied tightly around her tiny waist and she wore the typical slim jeans and gray t-shirt with the colorful red and yellow Papa's logo stretched across her chest. First, she served a small table of women – all young and giggling. They smiled and waved at the camera as the waitress bent down to get her smiling face in between two of them. Then they moved on to two men standing along the wall who also proudly posed with the lovely waitress as she served them their drinks. This continued until the waitress pulled out her order pad and pretended to write while she asked for John and Elizabeth's order. The three posed for the bartender with the camera. Then just for good measure, the bartender took a photo of the waitress with the group behind them before raising a hand of thank you and ambling off toward the bar. Megan slouched down on her bar stool hoping no one was watching him return the camera to her with a wink and a thank you for the bills she was sliding across the bar. Tactful, she thought. She waited for a group to come up to the bar for an order and then high tailed it out to the front door and to Joan's car. She drove around the parking lot just once to see if she spotted Edward's car again. Nope. It wasn't there, but as she was driving out to the highway she noticed the sleek green car parked in the street about a block down from Papa's lot. "Trying to be careful, are we?" she whispered to herself raising an eyebrow. Then just for good measure, she pulled in behind the green sports car and slid out the camera to take another photo of the back with the vanity plates clearly visible.

This trip didn't quite take the thirty-five minutes the first one had. There was no moon in the sky and everything seemed inky black and very cold. There was very little traffic, so she drove along quite comfortably. Arriving back at the studio, the parking lot was still filled with staff cars when she pulled in. Rehearsal must still be on, she thought. Gently pulling off the stocking cap and fluffing her spiky hair again, Megan resumed her impeccable appearance as she quickly shed her heavy winter coat at the coat rack in the front of the reception area. She snatched Joan's camera from the front pocket of her coat before scampering back to Joan's office. People were just starting to amble out of the back ballroom with tired but satisfied expressions on their faces. Clive Forbes seemed in better spirits. He was giving some "good job" comments to several of the dancers as he strutted out with Donnette Hubble clinging to his arm. She was the ever cheerful girl next door with her preppy skirt, cardigan sweater and fluffy blonde curls surrounding her dimpled cheeks.

"How about a quick trip out to Papa's to survey the floor?" Clive was calling to Tommy. "It's not too late yet." Tommy glanced at Molly who shrugged and nodded. "Great!" Clive chimed. A few more of the staff decided to make the trip as well, and they all headed quickly out the door for the country western club.

Joan stood in her doorway with her reading glasses slipping down her nose and a look of concern on her face as Megan took her by the crook of the arm and led her back inside her office. "Well?" Joan finally asked when they closed the door and made sure the staff was well enough away from the office door to hear any of their conversation. She folded her arms across her chest and waited for the news.

"I got the photo. Yes, he was there again with the Elizabeth looking person who I'm sure is our Elizabeth as I spotted Edward's car parked once again along the street about a block from Papa's." Megan placed the camera on the desk top and grinned.

"Did they know you had taken the picture?" Joan's face was lined with worry.

Megan told her the story of the bartender, and Joan's face softened. She smiled and nodded. "Good! That's very good. I was so worried about you. We don't know what kind of man John Jones is nor do we know how he is involved. But if he is involved, it could be in a murder investigation. Not a very good person to have angry I'm sure," Joan huffed. "Need a ride home? We'll take these photos to the detective in the morning and maybe he can tell us who this man really is." Joan wanted to get out of the studio quickly. Now that the staff had scattered, it wasn't a pleasant thought heading out to a cold car in a deserted parking lot if John Jones had any inkling they had a photo of him ready to hand over to the police. They both grabbed their coats and scurried outside carefully looking around searching for anyone who might be outside waiting to waylay them for any reason. But the parking lot was empty. Totally empty. Both Megan and Joan sighed in relief. The already warm car was a welcome to both as they slid into their seats.

XIV.

Joan had the photos blown up into glossy prints at the one hour photo shop just down the block from her house and then headed over to the police station. She had called early to make sure the detective was going to be in all morning. He was eager to see what she had for him. Joan sorted through the prints until she found the one of a pale Elizabeth Tomlinson and John Jones staring at the camera with a lovely waitress standing behind them note pad poised as if waiting for their order. It had been dark in Papa's, but the picture was clear and crisp. The bartender had done a superb job with all of the photos. She wondered if he were asked to do this same thing very often. He seemed to know just what to do when presented with the request.

The detective was in a short meeting, the officer at the desk told Joan when she arrived. Could she wait just a few minutes? Of course. Joan removed her coat – it was warm in the hallway lined with chairs. Her navy blue gathered skirt was a heavy wool and covered her crossed legs. The matching navy jacket was also quite comfortable. She wore a navy and white striped shell beneath along with a slender gold chain around her neck. There were no mirrors so she couldn't check her hair. She ran her fingers through the brown bob giving it a slightly fuller look. The gray streaks were hardly noticeable yet but she saw every hair whenever she caught sight of her image in one of the studio's many mirrors. That was the problem with working in a dance studio – so many mirrors! A headache for anyone concerned with growing old.

The detective came out of a side office and greeted her warmly before ushering her into one of the small conference rooms. "This is what I have," she plopped down the photo of John Jones and watched the detective study the couple in the picture.

"This woman here?" he pointed to the smiling tilted face poised behind the seated couple.

"Just a waitress. No one we know, I'm afraid," Joan answered back. He nodded and asked if he could have the picture to compare with mug shots of any known criminals. "Of course," Joan nodded. "It's yours. I just hope we can find a connection. It's all so confusing right now, and we'd love to get some answers."

"So would we," the detective leaned forward with a smile that was not particularly happy, just agreeable. Joan told him about her conversation with Donnette Hubble and pulled out her drawing from her purse. He studied this as well then asked if he could make a copy for himself.

"I can see why you were so interested in Clive Forbes," Joan commented. "He is the one who is the closest to Edward right before his death. Might I ask where exactly you found the dart? Was it on Edward's left side in the back?" The detective stared at her carefully and then nodded. "Clive was positioned perfectly, wasn't he?" Again the detective nodded.

"I don't want to believe it is Clive," Joan said softly. "I just don't want it to be true. And if it is him, I don't know why. Why would he do something like this?" The detective shrugged. Obviously he had no personal knowledge or interest in Clive Forbes. Not like Joan did. Not like the rest of the staff did.

"I'll probably try to bring him in for more questioning soon. Don't be concerned when I do..." he ventured slowly. "If it's not him, publicly taking him out of the studio might make the person who really killed Edward – if there is someone else – make a mistake. It will make them relax a bit and maybe do something or say something that will give us a clue." Joan nodded. Joan's face was drawn when she left the station and headed toward the studio.

The staff plus Mr. Nelson and Miss Hubble were already in practicing. They only had a few days to perfect a Two Step that hundreds of people would be watching. They were determined to make this routine something great. The back ballroom was filled with people in cowboy boots and country music twanging in the background. It was important to practice in the clothing they would actually be wearing the night of the routine to make sure it was comfortable worked with the planned dance movements.

Tommy was partnered with a downtown teacher because Anna wanted the tiny Molly to dance with Ashley. When Tommy spotted Joan stop at the front desk for messages and then shuffle across the small ballroom toward her office, he excused himself from his partner to have a word with her. She unbuttoned her coat as he stared at her providing some tidbits of news from last evening.

"I think Elizabeth was at Papa's last night when we arrived. She probably wasn't expecting we would be over there after rehearsal and let her guard down a bit. I was looking around for her as soon as we got in and there she was. But her back was to us again, and she left quickly. When I turned around again to find her after ordering a drink, she was gone. I mean gone, not seen again all night." He made his report in a whisper and then hurried back to the ballroom to continue his rehearsal. Joan smiled at his diligence. No one would know about the pictures. She and Megan had agreed to tell no one about that.

Elizabeth was early for once. She too saw the rehearsal in the back ballroom in progress and managed to open her door undetected and fling her fur onto a chair. How did she manage to look so beautiful when she was in the studio and so dumpy at Papa's? Joan shook her head. Elizabeth fluttered her ringed fingers in Joan's direction and twirled around in an expensive flower print designer dress with a full dance skirt. She slipped on strappy sandals in a colorful red color after shedding her over the knee designer boots.

"Something springy on a cold winter's day?" Joan commented trying to make pleasant conversation. Elizabeth frowned and then as if she suddenly got the joke began to laugh.

145

She tilted her head back and really let out a whoop. Her blonde bang flung back away from her dark lined eyes with the smoky shadow creasing the eyelids. Then she sauntered back into her office and watched the rehearsal from her office window. More private.

Joan was sitting at the front desk later that afternoon looking through the appointments for the day and the week when Tommy jogged past. "Coffee?" he asked as he passed.

Joan nodded and flipped him a dollar from the coffee fund kept in a top drawer at the desk. "Just cream," she reminded.

"I remember," he grinned as he left. A few minutes later, he returned carrying two tall coffees. Placing one on the top of the reception desk, he smiled again.

"Why are you so interested in following Elizabeth?" Joan asked suddenly curious. "Are you trying to clear your friend Clive?" She sipped from her coffee cup and gazed up at his face peering over the top of the tall desk.

"No, Clive and I aren't all that close," he admitted. Then looking around cautiously to make sure no one was in ear shot, he explained. "When Elizabeth first showed up with Mr. Garrett, she tried to seduce Clive and I one night after the studio was closed." Joan's face seemed a bit taken back by this admission. "I don't really think that's very ethical. Two timing Mr. Garrett like that. So I'd really like to see her caught for whatever it is she is doing or has done," he replied with an uplifted chin - moral and upstanding in his posture as he pulled up to his full height.

Oh, so noble, thought Joan then she looked him in the eye and said, "Sort of like what you and Molly are doing to her husband?" That caught him off guard, and he frowned with new resentment in his voice.

"It's not like that. Molly and her husband don't really have anything in common."

"So they're not really a couple? A married couple? It's so easy to make excuses for one's own behavior while finding fault with someone else's," Joan answered in a steady voice. It wasn't really her business but she knew she had to respond. "Have you met him?" she asked tilting her head to the side. "The husband?"

"No, he's not interested in dancing or the studio. As I said, they have nothing in common." She could tell he was rethinking his own words carefully.

"And you know this because..." inviting him to finish her sentence.

"Molly said so." His stubborn lower lip protruded a bit as he pronounced his answer. "And I believe her," he added with a pout.

"Before you go making a judgment, maybe you should be sure. Maybe you should meet him and find out for yourself," she suggested. "I have met him. And he's a very nice young man. I emphasize the word 'young' because he is barely out of his teens. And if they have nothing in common, maybe there should be a decision to separate or divorce before you make claim to something that isn't yours to claim." Tommy walked away stiffly but maybe with a few new ideas to mull over.

147

Tommy had been a help – a big help to Joan. She thought about what he told her about Elizabeth and her attempt to seduce the male teachers in this studio. Interesting. What does it have to do with Edward's murder? She could see how it affected Tommy, but how had it affected Clive? Did he just blow it off or did he do something about it? Was he enticed by Elizabeth's beauty? Or was she just another of the many women who came and went through Clive's magnanimous love life?

Kiki had been a limp dishrag the past week after the first day Clive had been released from jail. Joan hated to see Kiki in such a mood because it not only affected Kiki Mays herself, but the rest of the studio as well. She moped and whimpered and made their lives difficult. In addition, her lessons were less than the perfect ones she generally taught on her good days. Joan had been watching carefully all week to make sure her students were not suffering from her moodiness. Her last lesson had been painful to observe. Not once throughout the entire lesson did she smile or give her student a compliment. The student reacted with frustration. He walked past the desk with a clenched jaw and disturbing look in his usually sparkling eyes. Joan knew it was time to confront Kiki about what was going on in her mind.

Seated in front of Joan with a devil may care attitude clearly expressed, Kiki stretched out into a lounging position and waited. At this point she didn't care what Joan was going to say to her. Her focus was on the sorrow of her own life. Poor, poor me! This attitude had to be addressed before it mushroomed out of control.

"Ok. Tell me what's going on," Joan demanded as she faced Kiki.

148

"Whatever do you mean?" Kiki's sassy tone was uncharacteristic of the lovely dancer.

"Oh come on, Kiki. Don't give me this attitude. Your students are suffering from whatever is bothering you," Joan tried to lead her into a mature conversation. Would Kiki take the bait and open up?

"Then fire me!" No, Kiki hadn't decided to look at this logically at all. Emotion was suffocating her spirit.

"You know I won't do that," Joan pursed her lips. "I know you are having trouble with Clive again. I know you are upset that he was a suspect in Edward's murder. We already discussed this. So what is happening now? Give me the facts."

"The facts! You want the facts?" Kiki, normally quiet and subdued was now shouting. Her face was twisted in anger. "The fact is Clive is seeing Donnette Hubble, a student. It is and always has been against the rules, but no one does anything about it when it involves Clive. He is immune to punishment and rules, isn't he? He took her to Papa's last night after the rehearsal. If you hadn't invited her to join our little routine, she wouldn't so openly defy the studio regulations. That's what is wrong. Those are the facts!" Her voice continued to rise in angry frustration. "If Mr. Garrett were still here, he wouldn't stand for something like this. He would do something about it!"

Joan leaned back in her chair. So that is what was going on. Joan somehow calmed Kiki down enough to talk more about what had happened. Kiki thought when Clive was released from jail, he would be appreciative of her efforts to prove him innocent. But he had only paid attention to her that very first morning, then he was cold and distant to her. He had demanded she take him home that evening and hadn't told her why or what he was thinking or doing – nothing at all. He hadn't confided in her at all about Edward's death or why he was avoiding her. Then to discover he was seeing Donnette was too much to take. It was pure torture to watch them during rehearsals laughing and whispering with their heads together and their hands clutching. Joan nodded solemnly as Kiki spewed out the words and tears began to roll down her face in large drops onto her forest green cotton blouse collar. Joan knew how she felt, sort of. She had definitely not gone through the same exact events that Kiki experienced, but everyone knew what it felt like to love someone who didn't love back – a jerk. And Clive fit that profile to a T.

"Kiki," Joan began in response. "I am sorry you have had to go through this pain. And I will have to approach Clive and Donnette about this situation, because they are not exempt from following the studio rules. They are the reason we have the rules. It hurts everyone on our staff when someone is blatantly non-professional. It also hurts our students. So I will take care of this. Now, you my dear, must realize you are infatuated with a jerk. Clive is not worth the hurt and pain. He is not the man to make you happy. So as hard as it is, you need to move on with your heart. Find someone else and not let him rip you apart. It has happened over and over. You are not learning from your mistakes. You are following the same path again and again. So how can I help you get past Clive? How can we get your life back to productive and happy? He's not worth the pain!"

Kiki sat back and blinked. So direct. So to the point. She was surprised and hadn't expected this. Her mind had been on one track and now it was slowly moving beyond to another track. Joan was snapping her out of this fog – this one glaring obsession that was driving her in an unproductive way. Kiki was smart enough to know this, but not strong enough to work it out herself. She knew she needed help. "OK. I need help. Give me the help I need." Her voice was soft and accepting. "I need it now."

XV.

Were they ready for the show? Yes. Costumes had been tried during the dress rehearsal and all was set for Papa's. The newer staff had the usual nervous anticipation and the seasoned staff was enthusiastic knowing they had a great and polished routine to perform.

Joan had pulled Donnette Hubble and Clive Forbes into her office for a brief but direct reprimand. Donnette seemed unaware that such a no fraternization rule applied to her, but she did after Joan confronted her. Clive was none too pleased but put on his best scowl and then his "sorry" face when Joan reminded him subtly that he was still the number one suspect in Edward Garrett's murder, and he would need the support of friends if he thought he could make it past the police suspicions. Joan smiled knowing Clive wasn't dumb enough to ignore her warnings.

Walking out of her office after the confrontation, Joan held her head high – in a valiant and assured manner – toward the reception desk. On to the next matter at hand.

"Cancel the last lessons of the day," Joan told the receptionist. "We need the time to get out to Papa's for the show.

Can you get these people in at other times? Earlier possibly?" The receptionist nodded with a grin as the two of them poured over the schedule. "Sorry I didn't think of this sooner," Joan apologized with a twist of her mouth. There had been too many things to deal with – too many things on her mind.

The group dressed in the studio and divided up into car pool groups. "Music? Do you have the music?" Joan reminded as they started to leave. Anna Smith grabbed the music at the last moment and raced out to join her group.

"Aren't you going?" Megan Meeker asked as she slipped into her coat.

"Yes, but a little later. I want to see the routine, but I have some work to finish up. Want to ride with me?" Joan looked up from the paperwork she was trying to finish. Megan nodded. They were now alone in the studio. Elizabeth once again scurried out early. The receptionist had begged a ride with one of the groups so she could meet friends and see the routine as well. It was quiet. Scary quiet.

Megan slouched in one of Joan's chair, coat draped over the arm and waited. The phone rang crisply breaking the last few moments of unusual silence. Joan looked up from her work and sighed. Every time she got a late call, it was something new to think about. She grabbed it on the second ring. "Studio. How can I help you?"

She listened carefully and reached for her scrap of paper for notes. "Yes, what was that again?" She scribbled furiously. "Don't worry, we'll be careful."

Megan could barely contain herself. What was it? What had happened?

"I'll tell you in the car. We gotta go if we want to see that routine." Joan reread the scrap of paper and snatched her coat from the chair. She snapped up her keys and shooed Megan out the door. Locking the door, she glanced around the mall hallway nervously.

"What's wrong? Why so jumpy?" Megan noticed the fear in Joan's eyes and began to feel uncomfortable.

"I am so glad you are with me. The detective called, and they have a name for us on your photo. His name isn't John Jones, but John Thomas. They call him 'Jonny Tom'." Joan unlocked the car door and slid into the driver's seat. Megan tossed the pile of photos from Papa's into the back seat so she could sit down.

"What do you mean they call him 'Jonny Tom'?" Megan buckled her seatbelt and waited for the car to warm up as she rubbed her fingers.

"He's a grafter - a con artist who makes money off of innocent people. The police are very surprised he is here in Minnesota. It's not really a hot bed for rich people. Especially now in the winter, that is for sure. Most of our wealthy are in warm places during these months. Florida or Arizona or California. Those are the places grifters like to frequent. Not Minnesota!" The car began to warm, and Joan put it into gear for the ride to Papa's. "He told us to be careful. We don't know why he is here or who his victim could be, but we don't want him to know we are in the middle of his con. That would be dangerous

153

for us." Megan nodded with eyes bugging out. "Dangerous," she repeated.

"How do they know he's in the middle of a con?" Megan asked quietly.

"Grifters are always in the middle of a con," Joan answered back with a sigh and a tightly pressed grimness to her lips.

They found a place to park at the back of the parking lot. As they locked up the car, both scoured the lot for the old rusty car driven by Jonny Tom. They sighed in relief when they didn't spot it any place.

"Boy, quite a crowd tonight," Megan commented looking around at the full lot. "Nice night for a show."

Papa's was full. The dance floor was full and those leaning on the bars were squeezed in tightly even in the huge open spaces available. Joan and Megan looked around for the staff. They were in a back corner readjusting shirts and boots. Standing along the edge watching and chatting with the group was the lovely Elizabeth. She was still dressed in her elegant designer floral print dress and strappy shoes. How had she managed to get across that icy parking lot without tripping and falling on her face? She seemed so tall, so slender, so model-like – so unlike the plain and simple Elizabeth person they had observed prior to this at Papa's.

When they were announced, the floor cleared allowing for an opened space in the center of the huge dance floor for the studio dancers. They walked on with precision and got into formation. When the music started, they began the routine. The crowd cheered and clapped especially when they did their side lift.

Everything was perfect. Everyone looked great – and they knew at the end of the routine they had done it the best they could. They left the floor and gave each other hugs before people in the audience surrounded them with congratulations and questions about learning to "dance like that". The event had been a success, not only for the dancers' esteem but for the studio. The new interviews would skyrocket this week, Joan predicted. She reminded herself to get into the studio early to field the phone calls that were sure to come in. The night was electric. It was so appropriate. The last time the studio staff was here as a group, they had experienced the worst. A death. This time, Papa's had redeemed itself. They had experienced the best. A win – a success.

Megan informed Joan she didn't need a ride home. She was riding with Tommy. Molly was riding back with one of the downtown teachers. Joan smiled. Maybe her little chat with Tommy had actually done some good. Maybe he had thought about his relationship with Molly and decided to make changes.

"Ok. I think I'll leave early then," Joan said. "I'll have to get into the studio early to finish up my paperwork, and I'm tired! Too much happening this week." She cheerfully waved to Megan and headed out to the parking lot. She carefully picked her way through the icy grooves made by the truck tires and found her car surrounded by two jacked up pickups. Fishing out her keys, she couldn't wait for the warm air to hit her face when she turned the heat to MAX.

Juggling purse and squeezing between the truck and car, Joan managed to slide carefully into the car and adjust the rear view mirror. For some reason, it was tilted down. As she raised the mirror into position, she saw the shadow in the back seat. There was a man seated in behind her. It was dark, but Joan knew it was Jonny Tom. She froze with her arms to her side. He hissed in her ear, "What are these my lovely?" He had the photo pile from Papa's in his hand and she could feel and hear the crisp sheets as he whipped them in the cold brisk air. "Thought you could find out about me, did you? Is that why the cops hauled me in for questioning today? Was it you who called them?" The voice was hard and menacing in its cruel softness.

Joan closed her eyes and shook – and not from the cold. She was so scared. What would this man do to her? He was clearly angry. How had he gotten into her car? Joan waited for him to touch her, grab her, or put a weapon to her head. Waited. And waited. There was silence. She hated the silence. It was made her nervous. Opening her eyes, she glanced into the rear view mirror. There was no longer a dark shadow. She turned her head reluctantly. Where was he? He was no longer in the back seat. The photos were gone, and he was not there! Was he Houdini? How had he escaped? She heard nothing. All was sickening silent – all was bitterly cold.

It took her about five minutes before she finally turned the key in the car to start up the motor with clammy shaking hands. She let it run, carefully locking her doors – as if that would do any good. He had gotten in without her key. He was clever. Then she drove straight to the police station. The detective in charge of Edward's murder would not be there this late. But she would tell them what happened. Would it save her from further harassment? She doubted anything could save her now. Jonny Tom knew she had given his photo to the police. He had found the other pictures in her car. How stupid of her not to destroy the other photos, or at least hide them so they weren't visible from any roving eye who passed by.

The policeman sat patiently taking her statement. He was kind but didn't fully understand the implication of this event. He didn't know about Edward's death, and the idea that this Jonny Tom could somehow be involved was something that was a stretch. Who knew if Jonny was even in Minnesota when Edward was killed. There was no evidence connecting one to the other. She would call again in the morning and hopefully reach the detective in charge of the investigation. He would know what she was saying – what she was afraid of. She went home but didn't sleep. And she needed rest so badly. But she couldn't stop thinking he would find her. If he could get into her car, he could get into her house. She huddled under her covers and rolled restlessly all night until the first crack of sun pulled her from her bed to stand in a hot steamy shower and finally snatch a cup of strong coffee. Her eyelids sagged, and she felt a weariness that made each step seem like death march.

Joan went into the studio early. There was nothing else to do. The only positive was it was daylight. In spite of the cold, the sun was actually shining. When the sun shone – no matter the season – it was time to rejoice. Joan did look around carefully to see if anyone was following her. When she sat comfortably in her office with her attentions toward the front of the studio watching for any uninvited intruders, she lifted the phone and called the detective. He was quiet as she described the man sitting in her car holding the photos taken two nights ago. She told him how frightened she was. There was silence. Then he informed her they had taken Jonny Tom into custody last night after her visit to the station.

"The policeman you spoke to called me immediately after you left, and I knew we had to do something. That man might be very dangerous. We couldn't take that chance. So we sent out a patrol car to arrest him. He's here now. You are safe for the moment," the detective explained.

"For the moment?" Joan voice pitched nervously. She didn't like the sound of that.

"We'll charge him with breaking and entry or harassment. Pretty minor charges. Who knows when he'll get out on charges like that," he tried to tell her the truth of the matter. "But he's not talking. And he's not telling us anything about the woman he was with in the photo. So who knows if she is really Elizabeth Tomlinson or not. If she is, she might be his mark. He might think she is wealthy now that Edward is dead. She might be a victim."

Joan had a hard time believing Elizabeth could be a victim, but she had to admit it was possible. Widows and soon-to be widows – as was Elizabeth's case – were easy victims. They needed a shoulder to lean on. Someone to confide in when feeling a loss. It was just Joan hadn't noticed Elizabeth feeling very much sorrow when Edward died. She almost felt relieved to think Elizabeth might be an innocent victim instead of a black widow.

The phone began to ring, and Joan found herself at the front desk fielding calls and scheduling appointments. After the successful show at Papa's last night, people wanted to learn to dance. The lines were all ringing, and Joan didn't have the opportunity to think about anything else but finding suitable times for the callers on those appointment sheets. When the staff came in, they were excited. Their faces lit up when they saw Joan with her reading glasses on chatting away on the phone and the other lines ringing. "Could you please hold," Joan said again and again. Megan ran into Joan's office to take some of the calls. There were runners checking back and forth on openings available so Megan could give out dates and times to her callers.

Elizabeth stalked in with a cool expression. No one noticed. She had on a crisp black suit with a slim skirt slit up the side and a pinched in waistline on the jacket. The low V in her blouse was a bright hot pink. Her lips matched the color of her top. The smooth slender line of her eyebrows was exaggerated and cruel. Her eyes were darkly shadowed in a smoky almost gothic look. She passed by the desk without anyone even looking up as she entered. Everything in the studio was busy – like a hive of buzzing bees. And the queen bee went by without so much as a blink of the eye from the worker bees.

When the receptionist came in to relieve Joan at the desk, she was able to pull Megan Meeker aside to tell her what happened in the parking lot at Papa's. Megan's face showed shock. She was the one who had the photo taken. She could have been the one Jonny Tom stalked and threatened. But the remaining pictures had been in Joan's car. Megan blinked her eyes. "Where is he now?" she gasped peering around uncharacteristically as if someone might jump out at any moment.

"Right now, he's in jail. But they don't know how long he'll be there before he gets out. It could be soon if he makes bail." Joan noticed Megan glance around the studio with quick furtive eye movements. "He's not here now. Trust me." Joan reassured her. "We would get a warning call if something like that were to happen." Joan hoped that was a true statement. No use worrying right now. They had a studio to run, and it was going to be a very busy studio if the phone calls this morning were any indication.

Joan walked to Elizabeth's door and knocked. It wasn't a dainty little rap, but rather a hard pounding knock. Elizabeth opened the door. Joan pushed past her and sat down waiting for her to join her. "The show last night was a huge success," Joan began.

Elizabeth smiled. "I know. I was there. Remember?" The remark was once again sharply barbed.

"We need you to step up to the plate," Joan continued.

Elizabeth frowned. She hadn't expected to hear this at all. She blinked and asked, "What do you mean? What do you want me to do?"

"Quite frankly, your job. You have been in the studio now for several weeks hiding in your office and sliding by. That won't work anymore. You need to do your job and interview all of these new students coming in. I will help you, of course, but you need to learn how to close a sale. I can't do it all. Megan will help as will Anna, but we are depending on you to pull your weight. And that starts today." No more to say, Joan rose and walked out leaving Elizabeth stunned and wide eyed. "By the way," Joan turned back as she headed out the door. "You look good today. Professional. You'll need to. You have interviews scheduled all afternoon and evening." Elizabeth's mouth flew opened. Her face paled, and she habitually flung her hair back away from her face. But her hands systematically stroked her suit front as if to put it into place – to prepare for her busy day.

The young receptionist was frantically waving her hand at Joan when she emerged from Elizabeth's office. Joan signaled back, "Do you need help with an appointment?" No, the receptionist shook her head. Then with hand signals pantomimed a phone call for Elizabeth. Joan nodded and popped her head back into the office. "Call for you," she announced.

It was way too busy, and Joan forgot about the phone call for Elizabeth. The staff sat around the table going over appointments. Everyone was booked solid. There would be no rest today for anyone. Megan, Anna, and Joan huddled together to plan who would interview who, what office could they use and just how they would pull everything off. Elizabeth emerged from her office, and the three of them waved her over. "We're planning the day's schedule. We need you and your office. So sit," Joan ordered. And she sat. Elizabeth put her head in with the rest of the group and took her assignments without argument. After decisions were made, Elizabeth pulled Joan aside.

Patiently waiting for her to speak, Joan toddled from foot to foot. The night of no sleep and busy morning of setting appointments was taking its toll on her. She was getting tired. She needed a coffee and quick. "That call," Elizabeth began, "was Edward's son." Her eyes began to cloud filling with tears. Emotion. This was a new look for Elizabeth. "I told him I didn't know when the body would be released so no plans had yet been made for the funeral. He seems nice. Said I should enjoy the condo and maybe I could take it after the funeral. Of course, I would have to continue with the payments. He said it had a hefty mortgage. I'll have to think about that." She looked steadily into Joan's eyes. "I just thought you would want to know."

Joan had never liked Elizabeth Tomlinson, and although that bothered her – disliking a person because of a gut feeling – it bothered her even more when there was a moment she did like her. And this was one of those moments. She shook her head. "Thank you," she replied in a calm steady voice. "Thank you."

XVI.

Coffee with the police detective was always pleasant. Joan took an hour to meet him in spite of the busy schedule. It was important. She arrived early as usual and took a sip of her coffee, watching the door for his familiar entrance and stomping of his feet. She smiled. There he was.

"We have a problem," he began before even ordering his coffee. Joan's interest was peaked as she waited for the reason for this problem. He continued. "We'll be releasing the body for burial next week, and we still have no answers. I'm afraid this case will go unsolved as soon as the funeral takes place. We can't keep people of interest around after that, I'm afraid."

"You mean Elizabeth?" Joan asked as they both nodded their heads in shared agreement. Yes, she knew that to be true. Why should Elizabeth stay around when she showed no interest at all in the studio? She was only coming in now each day because this detective had indicated he would be contacting her at the studio. He was a smart one, this detective.

162

He continued. "So I have a favor to ask of you. Actually a few favors," his voice trailed as Joan shook her head violently. The last favor had ended badly with a threatening experience. "I know you may be nervous – afraid – after the Jonny Tom incident. But we are not going to learn the truth unless you help us." She sighed, her shoulders sagging into what clearly could be termed as "poor posture". She rolled her eyes and then pulled up into professional mode.

Joan and the detective discussed the suspects briefly – there was still Clive Forbes who was present but had no known motive to kill Edward. And there was Elizabeth Tomlinson, the elusive fiancé who had possible motive but wasn't there. Who else? Certainly not Mr. Nelson. Not the Bells or Mr. Harrison. Donnette Hubble? What possible motive was there for the girl next door? Joan mentioned her conversation with Tommy McLaughlin where he confessed Elizabeth Tomlinson had tried to seduce both he and Clive. The detective raised an eyebrow at this. "Certainly, this doesn't change much," Joan added to the story. The detective was silent for a moment. Thinking. Pondering.

"I think we need to get Clive's side of this story," the detective suggested. "And we've had chat after chat with the man to no avail. But maybe you could get somewhere if you had a heart to heart with him. The problem is if he did commit this murder and the connection is tied to this enticement by Elizabeth, you could be in dangerous waters if you bring it up. So I am going to suggest we monitor your conversation."

"A wire?" Joan was suddenly intrigued. This was exciting. A real adventure. And she was right in the middle of it.

"That or a bug in your office. We could set up a monitoring station nearby. Maybe next door or in the back of the studio near the restrooms." He mulled over the possibilities and nodded slowly. "Yes, that would work out. But before we do that, we need some information. We need the information from Elizabeth's office. Whatever that might be. She is too secretive for it to be nothing."

"We have tried and failed," Joan sighed. "I don't know how we can do this without a search warrant."

"Well, this is my plan," the detective continued to explain, and Joan nodded in agreement. It just might work. "We'll have to try later today," he said. "The sooner the better."

Joan groaned. "Today is so busy."

"We don't have much time left. We need that information to follow through on the investigation. You must be very careful and not move anything or she will suspect something is amiss." The detective waited for a response.

"I guess today will be no busier than any other day. That routine the staff did at Papa's has really brought in the business. It will be the same tomorrow and the next, so today is as good as any other. Ok," Joan agreed.

When Joan returned to the studio, the ballrooms were filled with new students and frantic teachers. Megan was using Joan's office for her interviews, and Anna was helping with chats on the lessons. Elizabeth was conducting one interview in her office when Joan arrived. How was that going? she wondered. When the interview was finished, Elizabeth escorted the student to the front ballroom for the lesson with Ashley. As she successfully passed off the student, the detective approached the front desk. He signaled for her, and she joined him in the reception area.

"I need to speak with you immediately," he said sounding rather urgent. His voice raised in an almost frantic manner. "Let's go have coffee."

Elizabeth's eyes showed a panic but she instantly changed the look to excuse. "I have a new student to interview in just half an hour," she said with a slight whine in her voice.

"Half an hour is perfect," he said firmly. Then he motioned for Joan to join them. "I will need Miss Tomlinson for about a half hour. She tells me she has an interview to complete soon. If we run over will you take over for her while she is gone?"

Joan nodded. "Of course. Whatever I can do to help!" Joan made sure to look surprised at the suggestion and watched as the detective took Elizabeth's elbow and led her out of the studio for a brief meeting.

As soon as they disappeared, she scooted into Elizabeth's now unlocked office. Where to look? What was she looking for? She began with the desk drawers. Luckily the drawers had been constructed with no locks or Joan was sure those would be locked as had been Elizabeth's office door. Nothing of importance in the drawers. She was frantic. She began to feel beneath the drawers and the top of the desk for something that could be taped to the bottom. Nothing. She felt under the chair. Nothing. But there was a plastic runner beneath the chair so it would roll on the carpet that seemed a little uneven. Moving the chair, she lifted the edge and spotted the folder. Pulling it out she checked to make sure

165

there was no tape or seal that would give Elizabeth a signal her papers had been tampered with. No. Nothing she could see. There were only a few sheets in the slim folder and little time left. She snatched the papers leaving the folder and raced to her office to make copies then returned the sheets just as they had been before she took them. Carefully sliding the copies into her bottom desk drawer beneath her own paperwork, she was standing with Elizabeth's student and Ashley when the detective and Elizabeth returned to the studio.

Elizabeth spotted Joan with her student and smiled with relief. The meeting had been about the funeral arrangements and the release of the body – not about a suspect in the murder. She joined the three on the floor and invited the student to return to her office for a final chat. Joan asked if she would like her to join them, and Elizabeth smiled. "Yes of course."

The student bought a few more lessons and walked away with a smile and a step of excitement. Joan turned to congratulate Elizabeth on an interview well done then added, "I didn't want to step on your toes by asking to join you, but I knew it was your first official interview close and thought you might want a little support." She flashed her a big smile and excited little clap of congratulations. That put Elizabeth at ease, and she eagerly joined Joan at the front desk to recheck her schedule for the day.

"Once you get one sale under your belt, it's so much easier," Joan was explaining to her. "What did the detective need? Has there been any progress in the investigation?" Joan feigned ignorance and tried to seem as curious as she could.

"They are releasing Edward's body for burial next week, so I need to contact his parents and son about funeral arrangements. He gave me their contact information and told me what the autopsy revealed." Elizabeth's lips pressed together.

"What? What killed Mr. Garrett?" Joan's eyes widened. She hoped her expression was one of intense interest.

"Poison." Elizabeth pronounced the word carefully.

"Oh, my. Was it in his drink? Food?" Joan showed appropriate surprise.

"No. He was stabbed with a dart. A very small dart!" Elizabeth stated as if she hadn't known before this very moment. Her voice was very smart and to the point as she nodded while presenting her newly acquired information.

"What? That is so bizarre. Bizarre!" Joan shook her head, eyes widening in shock and surprise. The conversation with Elizabeth had drawn her into a comfortable confidence. Elizabeth was almost eager to have someone to unburden the tale. Now she seemed completely caught up in the activity and the chaos of the studio as well. Hopefully this would distract her from any worry about her opened and unattended office. It seemed to work for the moment. Now Joan would have to get those papers to the detective. And as soon as possible.

Elizabeth had another interview scheduled right away. The student was already sitting in the reception area. "Do you want any help on this?" Joan asked nodding toward the older man in the comfortable chair nervously tapping his feet.

Elizabeth smiled and shook her head. "I think I can do this, thanks." Her voice was sugary and confident. She walked over to introduce herself and escort the man to her office. Joan sprinted to her own office and uncovered the copied pages in her drawer. Tucking them into her skirt waistband and covering them with her oversized tunic top, she walked out of the studio and into the mall hallway to slip them to the waiting detective. Task done. Now to determine what the papers would tell them about Elizabeth Tomlinson. If anything.

After an extremely busy day, Joan Ericson brought the staff together for an impromptu meeting at the end of the last lesson. "Only five or ten minutes, I promise," she pleaded as they turned tired faces at the request. "Thank you everyone for an extremely gallant effort on a very chaotic day. Let's congratulate Miss Tomlinson on four new student sales." They all turned to clap as Elizabeth smiled and bowed. "Advanced teachers! We need to use you in the future for some new student lessons. We are just too busy and need to somehow get everyone scheduled. We also have the Las Vegas competition coming up. So I am going to ask each advanced teacher to meet with me tomorrow morning before dance session for a review of your student list and determine who will be going to Las Vegas for the competition. Clive," she pointed to a sullen Mr. Forbes who seemed very eager to get out of the studio, "I will meet with you first. Nine o'clock sharp!" He groaned but nodded. "Miss Mays, ten o'clock. Mr. McLaughlin, eleven, and Miss Ross, eleven thirty. Tommy and Molly, you have a few advanced students, but because you teach new students as well, your list should be rather short – hence the shorter time for your meetings," Joan barked out the assignments and then excused everyone for the evening after another round of applause for a job well done. Evening over. Or so she thought.

After making sure she had an escort to her car and checking the back seat carefully, Joan drove home through the cold evening only to spot a patrol car at her house. Oh, no. What could be wrong now?

"Sorry to bother you, Miss Ericson, but I was given instructions to make sure your house was safe before you enter this evening." The patrolman tipped his hat with a smile. The skin around his eyes crinkled with signs of stress and age.

"Safe? Why wouldn't it be?" she demanded. Joan's eyes careened around her front yard to see if anything was amiss. Any new foot prints other than the mailman? Windows? Doors? All seemed intact and undisturbed.

"Just a precaution," he assured her tipping his hat again. She tramped up to the front door with the officer directly behind her. After unlocking the door, she gestured for him to enter. He raised his hand indicating she should wait on the front stoop. She shivered wrapping her arms around herself and looking over her shoulder periodically. Had they released Jonny Tom already? Otherwise, why the concern? To make matters worse, the officer pulled his gun from its holster as he cautiously peered around the corners before entering. She sucked in the cold crisp air and stared out into the darkness of her front yard. The street light seemed to blaze with unusual brightness as she followed the lines of the dark bushes edging her property. Maybe it was just the darkness, but everything seemed to move, waiver, and shift in shape.

The officer emerged with a thumbs up. "All Ok," he nodded but then added, "Detective Moran said to expect a call from him this evening. I'm calling in now to let him know the house has been checked, and you are home." He turned from her and sauntered back to the patrol car. She instantly wanted to call him back – tell him not to leave her alone – but her words wouldn't come out of her mouth. She clamped her lips together tightly and peered into her house.

Joan was tired, and now she was cold. She stomped her feet and scurried in relocking the door behind her. Now he was scaring her. And what was this call about? The phone rang before she even had time to shed her coat.

"Yes?" she answered. "You scared me with that officer searching my house. What's happening? Should I be worried?"

The detective outlined the procedure they would need for tomorrow morning – the wired interview with Clive Forbes. He would meet her at the studio at eight am sharp to set up the equipment in the back bathroom area. Ok. Ok. And now for the reason they were patrolling her house. What? They were patrolling her house?

"Yes," the detective's voice didn't sound too worried. "Those papers you gave me...there was a marriage license and a birth certificate among other insignificant papers. But those two gave us a bit of a concern."

Joan waited. "Why were you concerned?" Her heart began to pound as her voice lowered.

"Elizabeth's real name is Elizabeth Thomas or as she is known in our system, Betsy Thomas. She is John Thomas' wife."

So Jonny Tom was Elizabeth's husband? "That must have been why Elizabeth was so concerned when Edward announced they were getting married so quickly," Joan's mind was churning. "She was already married and that might cause problems legally when they filed for a license. So she was – is – a grifter too. And Edward was her mark – her victim. She was collecting jewelry and clothes and who knows what else. Of course, she can't leave the studio until after the funeral or the whole relationship will come under suspicion not only by the studio staff but by the police."

"You've got it! Elizabeth is a whiz at picking locks and other such tricks. That's how Jonny got into your car. That's how Elizabeth was able to lock her office door. And that is why we are watching your house. If Elizabeth suspects you found those papers she might, just might, try to search your house for the evidence. But don't worry, we're on the job. We'll be watching you all night." He sounded reassuring. Was she reassured? Not one bit.

"Do you think Elizabeth – Betsy and Jonny – were involved in Edward's murder? I think that would have been foolish. They had nothing to gain by killing their mark. Unless Elizabeth went through with the marriage and became the beneficiary on his studio or insurance policy, there would be no reason to kill him. I haven't heard she's getting any insurance money – not with his parents and son." Joan threw out her theories freely. "And I really think she was surprised when I told her about Edward's death. She truly showed shock."

"You aren't growing fond of our Miss Lizzy, are you?" the detective sounded curious and teasing.

"Oh, no. She's still a thief and a liar. But she seems to have softened a bit. I just don't know who the real Elizabeth is yet. I don't know if I ever will see the real person." Joan sounded a bit sad at this lost person but still wary.

"And you should be very careful. We still haven't ruled those two out as suspects. We still don't know if Jonny might have been in the club that night even if Elizabeth wasn't. We'll have to check that out. Pass around his photo to some of the patrons for identification. Who knows why he might try to murder Edward? Although it seems the method would not be in his character. Poison? Not really Jonny Tom's style."

"Why do you think the two of them always met at Papa's? That seems like a strange place with so many people who might recognize Elizabeth?" Joan had been playing with that question for a long time. And now that it was determined the woman in Jonny's company at the club was actually Elizabeth, she was even more confused by the choice.

"I don't know. We'll have to ask them when we arrest them." He sounded matter-of-fact.

"Arrest? You're going to arrest them?" Joan hadn't thought about that. "Even if they aren't involved in Edward's murder?"

"They stole from Mr. Garrett and misrepresented themselves. At least Elizabeth Tomlinson – Thomas – did. That's fraud. She's a grifter Joan and will just move on to some other

innocent victim when she leaves. Do you want that to happen?"
He went through the facts of the situation.

Joan pondered all he said and had to agree. She couldn't
let someone else suffer. She found in spite of her reluctance to like
Elizabeth, she still was much too trusting a person just as Edward
Garrett had been. He had trusted a woman because she was
beautiful and interested. But had that been his downfall or was it
something else?

"Get some sleep, Miss Ericson. I'm meeting you at the
studio at eight o'clock. Are you prepared for the discussion with
Mr. Forbes?" The detective was signing off. Joan yawned and said
she was crystal clear on her meeting intentions and signed off
feeling secure the patrols were watching her house for a
comfortable and much needed night of sleep. That bed right now
looked like heaven on earth.

Seven o'clock came too soon. But Joan peered around her
dark bedroom to make sure she was alone. Yes, all seemed good.
She ran through her questions for Clive as she showered and
dressed for the studio. What was she trying to pull from him?
And how was she going to get those answers? Was she nervous?
Yes. But she was a trained and successful interviewer. Now was
the time to use all of those talents to extract the information the
police needed regarding this murder.

Dressed in a black flowing tunic and long slim black skirt,
Joan patted her hair into place and carefully checked her make-up
as she passed the first mirrored wall on her way to her office. The
detective was trailing behind her with another uniformed officer
carrying a case over his shoulder. The uniformed policeman

walked right past her as she opened her office door to find a perfect location for his equipment near the back restrooms. Women's bathroom? Possible.

The detective looked around as she opened her door and flung her coat on a chair in the corner. He surveyed the desk and chairs to find just the right place for his concealed microphone. Joan began to feel nervous. In her mind she reviewed her speech, her questions and her assignment.

"Don't worry," the detective purred. "We'll be right here monitoring everything. You are safe."

"I'm not worried about safety," Joan sighed. "I'm worried I may not ask the right questions. I'm worried I may not get the right answers."

He smiled back at her – a smile of trust and assurance. "Well, I don't want to scare you or put more pressure on you but we checked out Jonny Tom carefully. He has an alibi for the night of Edward Garrett's murder. He wasn't even in the state. It's a pretty solid alibi. So this could be a very important conversation." Joan sighed. Great!

Joan put some coffee on in the small kitchenette and surveyed the set up in the tiny bathroom. Two men squatting in there listening to her conversation could be quite humorous. She chuckled. She only wished she could take a picture of that cramped scene. The coffee gurgled invitingly, and she poured a cup for herself and wandered back to her office, closing the French doors to the back ballroom so Clive would not become suspicious of any activity in the back of the studio.

Clive Forbes was prompt but looked as if he had slept somewhere else last night. His oversized linen sport jacket was rumpled, and his hair distractingly hung over his forehead in an oily curl. He was tall and swarthy normally. Today he looked haggard and hunched – his lean body seemed even more gangly than usual. It was that vibrant energy he normally injected into the studio that he lacked this morning. Frankly, he was a mess.

"Too early for you, Clive?" Joan teased. Get him in a more talkative mood, she decided immediately. Be light and cheerful. Laugh a bit.

"Late night, last night," he admitted slumping in the chair across from her desk and dropping his pile of lesson plans and papers on top. "But I suppose this is necessary…".

"Coffee?" she offered. "And yes, it is necessary I'm afraid." More than you could image was the next thought that popped into her head. She flashed a smile in his direction and chewed on her lower lip.

"You know I never touch the stuff," he grinned at the coffee question. "But it does smell good this morning. Another couple of nights like this one, and I may have to change my habits."

"Ok," Joan slapped her palms down on her desk in a "let's get down to business" gesture. "Let's go over your list of students. Start with Donnette Hubble. What do you want to do with her? We really need teachers now with the Papa's customers pouring in for lessons – especially talented young dancers able to handle new students. She would be perfect."

"You and Mr. Garrett!" he responded with frustration and a quick shake of his head. "She is my best competition student. Or at least she could be. She hasn't been here long enough to even try competing. I want to save her for some big performances in Las Vegas. She's my ticket to the big time in this business."

"Speaking of 'big time in this business'," Joan pawed through paperwork on her desk before finally coming up with the paper she was looking for. "Did you know your teaching hours and sales this last quarter qualified you for a top teacher award nationally?" She turned the paper around to face Clive. It was a list of the honor roll for the top teachers. His name was highlighted in yellow about a fourth of the way down the list. "Not bad for someone who has only taught dancing for about two years. Not even that!" Joan flipped her hand nonchalantly as she tried to figure out the time span in her head. "Certainly something to be proud of."

Clive Forbes stared at the paper and ran his finger down the list. He recognized the names above his as prominent nationally known dancers and a crooked smile crossed his face. His tired dragged out attitude suddenly changed to one of renewal. His vitality returned, and he sat up straight in the chair with a twisting grin crossing his face.

"Now that I have your attention," Joan continued with a smirk, "I need to know if you are having an affair with Donnette Hubble. Because if you are, there could be problems in the competition department. I would really have to seriously consider asking her to join our staff."

Clive's face lit up rather than the pout she had expected to see. "Nope. Absolutely not!" he triumphantly announced. "There was a time I considered it. She's cute and all, but not really my type. Too cheerleader-like. Chipper and annoying to be truthful."

"And since when did you have a type?" Joan teased again. "I thought you and Edward shared a love of women – any type of woman."

Clive's mouth gaped as he scratched his oily head. "I suppose you are correct there. We both do love our women. Or at least Mr. Garrett did love his women," he clarified quickly. "But I'm getting pickier in my old age." He slouched comfortably in his chair and flashed her a devious look as he peered over dark almost touching eyebrows.

"Old age? You can't be more than twenty-two years old!" Joan leaned back and looked at Clive. She knew he was younger than he looked. His hair was already beginning to recede and his face showed the signs of stressful living with lines beginning to form around his eyes and mouth.

"Actually, I'm only twenty-one," Clive admitted. "But I'm learning my lessons the hard way."

"What? The Kiki situation?" Joan prodded.

"Yeah, that's been very stressful. Kiki Mays is a very clingy person. She's made my life a bit awkward these past few weeks. I never promised her I would be exclusive. She just assumed things that could never be. I'm a guy who needs to be free. On the move with the relationship stuff." He nodded his shaggy head with a grimace of his mouth.

"Oh, I understand completely. I always knew that about you. You have to have lots of relationships." Joan nodded right along with him. Humor him, humor him.

"But not with students. Not any more at least," Clive clarified with a determined look in his dark shadowed eyes. His heavy black eyebrows closed in on the top of his beaked nose.

"Ok, confession time, Clive," Joan announced. "Tell me the truth about these affairs. Donnette, Kiki, Elizabeth?"

"Elizabeth?" Clive's mouth began to spread into a thin smile. "Yeah, I saw Donnette a couple of times outside the studio. She started to really believe we were a couple. But I put an end to that one real quick after our last talk and after I realized Edward wanted to make her a teacher. That would have been complicated to have both Donnette and Kiki in the same space fighting over me all the time. Anyway, I realized just what a great student Donnette could be after that last competition when I saw all of those other teachers with their winning students. Yeah, she would be annoying as a girlfriend but great as a competition partner. So I put a halt to that one quick enough. And Kiki…well she's a nut case. She just follows me around and attaches herself to me wherever I go. I can't get rid of her. It doesn't matter what I say or do. She doesn't give up. She's like a leach." Clive began to unburden his thoughts as if this was the first time he was allowed the time and space to do so. He continued. "Elizabeth? Yeah, she came on to me a couple of times. That was when she was engaged to Edward, too. She was really interested." He began to smile in a bragging sort of way. "She didn't want to marry the old guy, you know. But she didn't know how to get rid of him. She just didn't know. So I told her I would take care of things." Suddenly he stopped

178

short. What had he just said? Quickly, he changed the subject. "I'm just a freewheeling guy these days. I pick up a girl out at the club – someone different every night." He shrugged his shoulders with a gleam in his eye. He was now carefully selecting his words. Speaking slower and more deliberately with a new sneer in his attitude.

Joan nodded and went on with the rest of the interview. They went down the list of his other students and reviewed procedures for taking on new students. Joan's mind began to churn. Had this information been what the detective was looking for? Was it enough to feel Clive had something to do with Edward's murder? She didn't know. Just then she spotted Kiki Mays standing outside her door. She glanced at her watch. Was it already eleven o'clock? She had to dismiss Clive and get on to Kiki. Had she done the job? Only time would tell. Smiling at Clive she explained their time was done. They could get together later if there was something more they had neglected to cover. He should think it over during the day and let her know if they should review further.

Clive got up to leave and opened the door to come face to face with Kiki Mays. Her face was hard. She glared up at him as he reeled back. Turning his body to squeeze out the door, he slipped past her to let her enter. Kiki strutted in with a sulk on her face that did nothing to accentuate the beautiful gold toned dress she wore. The dress had a colorful Caribbean design with aqua and teal patches of beach scenes strewn across the skirt and sleeves. Her hair was neatly cropped again into a sophisticated fullness at her forehead and short on the sides. The make-up was applied perfectly. But that face. It was anything but happy.

179

She dropped into the chair and spread her paperwork out in front of her with tightly pursed lips. Her eyes never met Joan's searching face. There was something wrong. The steam was literally coming out of her ears.

"Kiki? What's wrong?" Joan begged.

"Nothing," Kiki shouted with a quick sharp tone. She began to list her students and her plans for each one with efficiency, a steely bite to her voice, and her lips pressed tightly together. Joan wrote notes on her own lists and bit hard on her lower lip. She asked no questions and simply let Kiki Mays ramble on with her own agenda.

Finally, when Kiki was finished, Joan stared intently into Kiki's flushed face and asked slowly the question she had been thinking all hour, "What is going on with you and Clive? And I want an honest answer here."

Kiki looked down before speaking. "I wanted Clive to be innocent. I really did."

"But?" Joan led her voice in a direction that begged her to continue. Her head cocked to the side – curious, listening, waiting.

"I just found out from Elizabeth Tomlinson how Edward died," Kiki pressed her lips together again. "A poisoned dart!" She spit out the last sentence with a tart crispness.

"When did she tell you this?" Joan frowned. She knew Elizabeth and Kiki were not two close friends who would normally share such information in a phone conversation or over early morning coffee. And Elizabeth had just found out about the manner of Edward's death yesterday – a busy day with little time for conversation.

"Just now," Kiki announced. "She followed me in from the parking lot. She needed someone to confide in, and I guess I was the one who was there with a sympathetic shoulder to cry on." Not that Joan could imagine Elizabeth crying on anyone's shoulder. And what was Elizabeth doing here in the studio so early? This was unexpected.

"I know that sounds gruesome but why does that upset you so much?" Joan prodded.

"You knew? You knew he died from a poisoned dart?" Kiki demanded.

"Of course I knew. The police told me the cause of death. But what does that have to do with Clive?" Joan began to stiffen. Her shoulders shrugged.

"I saw that dart in his jacket pocket on the night we went to Papa's. It had a plastic cover over the tip. I thought it odd to have a dart in his pocket but I didn't think much of it until this very moment. Now I know he is guilty. I feel so foolish – I was the one who tried so hard to give him support and prove he was innocent. I couldn't believe he would do something like that. Why would he do it? Why?" Kiki was no longer angry but emotionally distraught. She was on the verge of hysterical tears – was it for her naïve nature or his true self exposed to her finally after so many months of hurt and pain?

"How did you manage to see the dart?" Joan asked with new curiosity and prodding.

181

"I guess I was jealous of Donnette. She was going to be at Papa's with the rest of the students. So I decided to spy a bit – check through his pockets for notes or whatever. I look through his desk and pockets most days when he's out teaching. Just to make sure. Who knows what I might find. I just had to know if he was faithful to me or not." Kiki's eyes welled with tears.

"Kiki, he was never faithful to you. Nor has he ever been faithful to anyone. So you are not alone," Joan whispered. She didn't know if this was the right thing to say right now or if it would make Kiki feel any better. It was just the truth. Kiki needed to begin to see the truth. Joan handed her a tissue and waited for the onslaught of tears to follow.

Scooping up her coffee cup, Joan left Kiki with her sorrow and a new box of tissues pushed in front of her. She opened her door and plodded back to the kitchenette to fill her cup and find the detective. Surely this new development was what he wanted – needed to solve this case. She was hoping he had listened in on this last conversation as well as the hour with Clive.

The two officers were huddled around their equipment in the tiny bathroom when Joan peered in. It was starting to feel very stuffy and warm in the small space. The air was moist and heavy.

"So did you get that?" Joan whispered softly.

"Get what?" the detective looked up. His ear phones were tight against his head and his eyes were straining as if listening closely to something.

"Kiki's information about the dart?" Joan answered thinking he was listening to the conversation – now over – in her office.

"We're listening to something else...". He signaled her with a pointed finger to be quiet and turned back to his equipment.

Joan shut the door and pondered. So they are listening to something else? What? She grabbed her coffee cup and wandered through the large ballroom to rejoin Kiki Mays. The long thin window along Elizabeth's office door was dark but there was slight movement inside. Had Clive gotten into Elizabeth's office and begun to search for something? What was he looking for? And where was Elizabeth? Kiki said she arrived at the studio with her.

Joan went up to the front desk and waited. She couldn't look into Elizabeth's office. She might be disturbing something that was going on. And she couldn't bear to go back inside her own office with a weeping Kiki Mays. It was just too much right now. So just stay put behind the reception desk and hope to see something as it happens. But what? What was happening?

Suddenly Elizabeth's door flew opened, and Clive backed out the door. His eyes were glaring and distraught. His shoulders hunched. He looked around behind him and seeing no one hissed, "You said we had a chance. You told me I was the one. You lying bitch."

"Oh, honey. You misunderstood me I'm afraid," Elizabeth cooed. She batted her eye lashes in a flirty fashion. "We never had a chance. You and me? Certainly not! I was just trying to get out of marrying Edward Garrett. When you said you would take care of things, I didn't know you meant to kill him!" Her voice went from soft and soothing to loud and accusing. Mocking. Her chin jutted out after the words spewed out of her mouth.

"How else was I going to take care of things? What else did you think I meant by that?" Clive sneered. "How dare you do this to me!" His head bobbed back and forth like toy.

Kiki Mays peered out the office door. Her face showed signs of shock – disbelief. Then flinging the door wide opened she demanded, "How could you do something like this for her." She pointed her finger at Elizabeth who was now leaning against the frame of the door in a seductive pose. Was this was Elizabeth's true nature? Taunting and cruel. Clive lunged for Elizabeth with a demonic scowl, but the policeman in the uniform leaped through the French doors and grabbed his wrists twisting them behind his back. Clive Forbes was startled and collapsed weakly against the wall.

Elizabeth relaxed and looked around frantically as if she were about to faint. She fanned her face with an opened palm. The detective emerged from the back ballroom and nodded toward her. "Nice job," his face showed no signs of joy. His expression was hard and almost mournful. It was not easy to solve a murder. Nor was it pleasant.

Kiki quickly rushed toward Clive in a mother-hen sort of way. No longer angry, she was now protecting him. Again. Reverting back to an emotion of disbelief, she wanted so badly for him to be innocent. The detective intercepted her before she could reach Clive and cradled her in his arms. Knowing, yet not understanding what she was going through.

Clive was led out to the waiting patrol car – head down, wrists clasped behind his back. The detective remained to settle Kiki into the chair in Joan's office once again with the box of tissues. He sauntered back toward Elizabeth still standing in her office doorway leaning weakly with her head thrown back. She was breathing heavily; her chest heaved up and down slowly as she inhaled and exhaled.

Joan had moved out into the small ballroom and was taking in all of the action. Her head snapped from one scene to the next. First, Clive and Elizabeth's dramatic conversation, then Clive's arrest, Kiki's break down, and now the detective approaching Elizabeth.

"So are we cool?" Elizabeth said with a toss of her hair. Her face was without emotion. Head tilted to the side, she leaned lazily against the door frame. Regaining control as usual. She was back to normal.

"Yeah. We got it all down on tape. You and Jonny are free and clear on this charge. But I'm going to watch you carefully, and if I see you have tried to con another soul, I'll arrest you immediately. Your head will spin, I promise you. Understand?" The detective had made a deal with Elizabeth. Get a confession, and she and Jonny Tom would walk with no charges for fraud or extortion.

"Maybe I'll just stay around for the funeral," she said quietly with her head looking down, eyes on the floor. "No need to let Edward's parents or son know about this stuff. They deserve better than that."

She turned to Joan. "Do you need help around here for a few days until the funeral? I can still help out with interviews and stuff...", Elizabeth offered with a raise of an eyebrow.

"That would be great. We certainly do need help," Joan smiled. Unexpected. Pleasantly unexpected. She caught herself with a slight softening feeling toward this woman. Her stare tried to pierce the exterior of her flesh and see where that heart was beating. But the armor remained with its cool hardness not letting in the looks of those around her. Not letting in the emotion of the situation.

XVII.

The funeral for Edward Garrett was emotional for some and calming for others. Edward's parents were elderly and showed the pain of losing a child. Elizabeth dutifully helped them into their seats and showed just the right amount of sorrow, dabbing her eyes with a handkerchief frequently during the service. She allowed Edward's mother to lean into Elizabeth's sturdy shoulder for support as the final words were read from the Bible.

Edward's son was now a tall and lean man in his late teens. Joan remembered him as a child and was pleasantly pleased to see him now a grown man. He shared the combination of good looks Edward brought with the sharply chiseled features of his mother. It was a good mix. He was a handsome boy now entering adulthood. The tragedy of this situation would not be evident for quite some time to this son who had scarcely known his father in recent years. He only remembered the man he had known as a small child – the father who had proudly brought him into the

186

studio and taught him to call his elders with a "Mr." or "Miss" in his address.

Elizabeth greeted Edward's son with an embrace and nodded her head frequently as they whispered their condolences. She informed the son she would not keep Edward's condo, and he should sell it if he was planning to stay in California. He agreed. Her eyes lingered on his form with sadness as he turned and joined his grandparents in the receiving line after the ceremony was completed. Maybe Elizabeth Tomlinson has also experienced death and a loss in her short lifetime. She seemed to understand the pain he felt.

After the service, when the relatives had returned home and true to her word, Elizabeth disappeared. She just never showed up for work. Joan had expected it, but she regretted never asking the questions that remained. Why? Why had Elizabeth chosen Edward for her plan? Why had she and Jonny returned over and over again to the murder scene – Papa's? The only answer Joan could imagine was the country western bar had felt like home – wherever that might be. They somehow felt comfortable in the big barn like building with the large dance floor and the twang of the country music playing in the background. Sitting in the corner of the smoky bar looking out into the hazy darkness felt like home.

It was only a few short weeks before Anna Smith and Megan Meeker finalized the move into their new space. It would feel strange not to have the two and their students and staff squeezed into the suburban studio with Joan, Kiki, Ashley, Tommy, and Molly. Tommy had taken over teaching Donnette Hubble and was looking forward to a year of competition successes. Donnette seemed happy as well. Although shocked by the turn of events with Clive's arrest for Edward's murder, she somehow seemed almost knowing about his confessed guilt. Maybe she had also seen something she shouldn't have that night at Papa's. If she did, she remained quiet about that event.

The grand opening for the new studio was scheduled for a Friday evening. Joan and her staff arrived an hour early to get a feel for the new place. It was located in a one story newly built mall complex only a quick half a mile from downtown Minneapolis. Crossing the bridge that stretched over the river brought a feeling of elegance that was missing in the downtown area. Tree lined boulevards circled the structure with ample parking lots close to the entrance. The studio itself was straight ahead nestled in between a coffee shop on one side and a boutique on the other. The fragrant smell of coffee and tea was enticing and pleasant. At first impression, Joan praised Edward for his choice of studio space.

The space, however, was tiny. Very small. There was a beautiful glistening wood dance floor immediately upon entering. But it was circular and much smaller than the large ballroom in the suburban studio. The back of the dance floor was surrounded by a series of circular floor to ceiling windows which brought in lots of natural sunlight during the day. There was only a short wall in the front with mirrors, and the cramped offices were along the sides. Although small, the place was sparkling new and luxurious. Now to see if all of the students would fit.

Although it proved to be tight with students and staff from both studios crowding into the dance space, Anna and Megan were thrilled to have the new location. They hoped the mall would prove to be a successful draw for new students. They greeted everyone with enthusiasm and excitement – a new beginning. Joan looked around and smiled. She hoped Elizabeth Tomlinson was also excited about her new beginning. She had heard from the detective that Jonny Tom had been arrested again on drug dealing charges. Elizabeth was now free to pursue a new life if she chose. Joan hoped she had found something in this dancing business to propel her into a new opportunity. Hopefully something that utilized her talents in a positive and healthy way – a new life.

Joan settled back into her office. She didn't bother to move back into Elizabeth's abandon office that had once been Joan's pride and joy. Both that office and Edward's remained empty as if a memorial to people lost. The Papa's shows continued and the students seemed to pour in, so she usually had a busy daily schedule to keep up with. It had been weeks since the funeral and at times, it all seemed to have just been a bad dream. Joan pushed around the papers on her desk. It was always a bit messier than she hoped for. The manila packet with her name on it was propped on top, but for some reason it took her a few minutes to focus in on the envelope. Where had this come from? She slit the seal and pulled out a sheet of paper. There was a note pinned to the top. In careful letters were these words: "Thought you might want to see this." It was signed by the police detective. There was a newspaper clipping – a column in the obituaries from a small Oklahoma town. It was the notice of the death of one Elizabeth Thomas from a drug overdose. There was no picture accompanying the notice.

Country Two Step:

The Country Two Step is danced in a closed dance position with the man's left hand holding the lady's right hand at about eyelevel for the lady. The man's right hand can be placed either on the lady's left shoulder blade or higher close to the back of her neck. The lady stands in front of the man lining up with his right shoulder so her feet are placed along different tracks on the floor than the man's feet. The lady's right hand is placed in the man's left hand and her left hand is either on the man's shoulder (if he places his hand on her shoulder blade) or looped around his right elbow if he places the right hand close to her neck. The Two Step is danced counterclockwise around the dance floor with the man beginning by moving forward and the lady moving backward. The feet should shuffle along the floor rather than lifting the feet to step.

The timing is Slow (2 counts of music), Slow, Quick (1 count of music), Quick.

Basic:

Man's part – Forward left foot (slow), Forward right foot (Slow), Forward left foot (Quick), Forward right foot (Quick).

Lady's part – Back right foot (slow), Back left foot (Slow), Back right foot (Quick), Back left foot (Quick).

Turning the lady into shadow position:

Man's part – Forward left foot, Forward right foot, on the quick, quick the man continues to move forward but turns the lady by taking her right hand and changing it to his left hand. As she turns, he takes her left hand in his left hand placing the lady into a shadow position – both are facing the same direction with the lady on the man's right side.

Lady's part – Back right foot, Back left foot, on the quick, quick the man turns the lady to her right. She does a half turn ending on the man's right side facing forward. The lady's feet on the quick, quick turn are right back beginning the turn then left foot forward finishing the turn.

Basic forward in shadow position:

Man's part – Forward left, Forward right, Forward left, Forward right (timing remains the same – Slow, Slow, Quick, Quick).

Lady's part – Forward right, Forward left, Forward right, Forward left (Slow, Slow, Quick, Quick).